22.7.17

Roy

Please renew or return items by the date shown on your receipt

www.hertsdirect.org/libraries

Renewals and enquiries: 0300 123 4049

Textphone for hearing or speech impaired   0300 123 4041

Hertfordshire

D1340372

520 783 59 0

Mr HARRISON'S *Confessions*

ELIZABETH GASKELL

Published by Hesperus Press Limited

28 Mortimer Street, London W1W 7RD

www.hesperuspress.com

Mr Harrison's Confessions first published in 1851

First published by Hesperus Press Limited, 2014

Designed and typeset by Roland Codd

Printed in Denmark by Nørhaven, Viborg

ISBN: 978-1-84391-518-8

CHAPTER I

The fire was burning gaily. My wife had just gone upstairs to put baby to bed. Charles sat opposite to me, looking very brown and handsome. It was pleasant enough that we should feel sure of spending some weeks under the same roof, a thing which we had never done since we were mere boys. I felt too lazy to talk, so I ate walnuts and looked into the fire. But Charles grew restless.

'Now that your wife is gone upstairs, Will, you must tell me what I've wanted to ask you ever since I saw her this morning. Tell me all about the wooing and winning. I want to have the receipt for getting such a charming little wife of my own. Your letters gave the barest details. So set to, man, and tell me every particular.'

'If I tell you all, it will be a long story.'

'Never fear. If I get tired, I can go to sleep, and dream that I am back again, a lonely bachelor, in Ceylon; and I can waken up when you have done, to know that I am under your roof Dash away, man! "Once upon a time, a gallant young bachelor" – There's a beginning for you!'

'Well, then: "Once upon a time, a gallant young bachelor" was sorely puzzled where to settle, when he had completed his education as a surgeon – I must speak in the first person; I cannot go on as a gallant young bachelor. I had just finished walking the hospitals when you went to Ceylon, and, if you remember, I wanted to go abroad like you, and thought of offering myself as a ship-surgeon; but I found I should rather lose caste in my profession; so I hesitated, and, while I was hesitating, I received a letter from my father's cousin, Mr Morgan – that old gentleman who used to write such long letters of advice to my mother, and who tipped me a five-pound note when I agreed to be bound apprentice to Mr Howard, instead of going to sea. Well, it seems the old gentleman had all along thought of taking me as his partner, if I turned out pretty well; and, as he heard a good account of me from an old friend of his, who was a surgeon at Guy's, he wrote to propose this arrangement: I was to have a third of the profits for five years, after that, half; and eventually I was to succeed to the whole. It was no bad offer for a penniless man like me, as Mr Morgan had a capital country practice, and, though I did not know him personally, I had formed a pretty good idea of him, as an honourable, kind-hearted, fidgety, meddlesome old bachelor; and a very correct notion it was, as I found out in the very first half-hour of seeing him. I had had some idea that I was to live in his house, as he was a bachelor and a kind of family friend, and I think he was afraid that I should expect this arrangement; for, when I walked up to his door, with the porter carrying my portmanteau, he met me on the steps, and while he held my hand and shook it, he said to the porter, "Jerry, if you'll wait a moment, Mr Harrison will be ready to go with you to his lodgings, at Jocelyn's, you know"; and then, turning to me, he addressed his first words of welcome. I was a little inclined to think him inhospitable, but I got to understand him better afterwards. "Jocelyn's" said he, "is the best place I have been able to hit upon in a hurry, and there is a good deal of fever about, which made me desirous that you should come this month – a low kind of typhoid, in the oldest part of the town. I think you'll be comfortable there for a week or two. I have taken the liberty of desiring my housekeeper to send down one or two things which give the place a little more of a home aspect – an easy chair, a beautiful case of preparations, and one or two little matters in the way of eatables; but, if you'll take my advice, I've a plan in my head which we will talk about tomorrow morning. At present, I don't like to keep you standing out on the steps here;

so I'll not detain you from your lodgings, where I rather think my housekeeper is gone to get tea ready for you."

'I thought I understood the old gentleman's anxiety for his own health, which he put upon care for mine; for he had on a kind of loose grey coat, and no hat on his head. But I wondered that he did not ask me indoors, instead of keeping me on the steps. I believe, after all, I made a mistake in supposing he was afraid of taking cold; he was only afraid of being seen in dishabille. And for his apparent inhospitality, I had not been long in Duncombe before I understood the comfort of having one's house considered as a castle into which no one might intrude, and saw good reason for the practice Mr Morgan had established of coming to his door to speak to everyone. It was only the effect of habit that made him receive me so. Before long, I had the free run of his house.

'There was every sign of kind attention and forethought on the part of someone, whom I could not doubt to be Mr Morgan, in my lodgings. I was too lazy to do much that evening, and sat in the little bow window which projected over Jocelyn's shop, looking up and down the street. Duncombe calls itself a town, but I should call it a village. Really, looking from Jocelyn's, it is a very picturesque place. The houses are anything but regular; they may be mean in their details, but altogether they look well; they have not that flat unrelieved front, which many towns of far more pretensions present. Here and there a bow window – every now and then a gable, cutting up against the sky – occasionally a projecting upper storey – throws good effect of light and shadow along the street; and they have a queer fashion of their own of colouring the whitewash of some of the houses with a sort of pink blotting-paper tinge, more like the stone of which Mayence is built than anything else. It may be very bad taste, but to my mind it gives a rich warmth to the colouring. Then, here and there a dwelling-house had a court in front, with a grass plot on each side of the flagged walk, and a large tree or two – limes or horse chestnut – which sent their great projecting upper branches over into the street, making round dry places of shelter on the pavement in the times of summer showers.

'While I was sitting in the bow window, thinking of the contrast between this place and the lodgings in the heart of London, which I had left only twelve hours before – the window open here, and, although in the centre of the town, admitting only scents from the mignonette boxes on the sill, instead of the dust and smoke of — Street – the only sound heard in this, the principal street, being the voices of mothers calling their playing children home to bed, and the eight o'clock bell of the old parish church bimbomming in remembrance of the curfew: while I was sitting thus idly, the door opened, and the little maidservant, dropping a courtesy, said:

'"Please, sir, Mrs Munton's compliments, and she would be glad to know how you are after your journey."

'There! was not that hearty and kind? Would even the dearest chum I had at Guy's have thought of doing such a thing? while Mrs Munton, whose name I had never heard of before, was doubtless suffering anxiety till I could relieve her mind by sending back word that I was pretty well.

'"My compliments to Mrs Munton, and I am pretty well: much obliged to her." It was as well to say only "pretty well", for "very well" would have destroyed the interest Mrs Munton evidently felt in me. Good Mrs Munton! Kind Mrs Munton! Perhaps, also, young – handsome – rich – widowed Mrs Munton! I rubbed my hands with delight and amusement, and, resuming my post of observation, began to wonder at which house Mrs Munton lived.

'Again the little tap, and the little maidservant:

'"Please, sir, the Miss Tomkinsons' compliments, and they would be glad to know how you feel yourself after your journey."

'I don't know why, but the Miss Tomkinsons' name had not such a halo about it as Mrs Munton's. Still it was very pretty in the Miss Tomkinsons to send and enquire. I only wished I did not feel so perfectly robust. I was almost ashamed that I could not send word I was quite exhausted by fatigue, and had fainted twice since my arrival. If I had but had a headache, at least! I heaved a deep breath: my chest was in perfect order; I had caught no cold; so I answered again:

'"Much obliged to the Miss Tomkinsons; I am not much fatigued; tolerably well: my compliments."

'Little Sally could hardly have got downstairs, before she returned, bright and breathless:

'"Mr and Mrs Bullock's compliments, sir, and they hope you are pretty well after your journey."

'Who would have expected such kindness from such an unpromising name? Mr and Mrs Bullock were less interesting, it is true, than their predecessors; but I graciously replied:

'"My compliments; a night's rest will perfectly recruit me."

'The same message was presently brought up from one or two more unknown kind hearts. I really wished I were not so ruddy-looking. I was afraid I should disappoint the tender-hearted town when they saw what a hale young fellow I was. And I was almost ashamed of confessing to a great appetite when Sally came up to enquire what I would have. Beefsteaks were so tempting; but perhaps I ought rather to have water-gruel, and go to bed. The beefsteak carried the day, however. I need not have felt such a gentle elation of spirits, as this mark of the town's attention is paid to everyone when they arrive after a journey. Many of the same people have sent to enquire after you – great, hulking, brown fellow as you are – only Sally spared you the infliction of devising interesting answers.

CHAPTER II

'The next morning Mr Morgan came before I had finished breakfast. He was the most dapper little man I ever met. I see the affection with which people cling to the style of dress that was in vogue when they were beaux and belles, and received the most admiration. They are unwilling to believe that their youth and beauty are gone, and think that the prevailing mode is unbecoming. Mr Morgan will inveigh by the hour together against frock-coats, for instance, and whiskers. He keeps his chin close shaven, wears a black dress-coat, and dark-grey pantaloons; and in his morning round to his town patients, he invariably wears the brightest and blackest of Hessian boots, with dangling silk tassels on each side. When he goes home, about ten o'clock, to prepare for his ride to see his country patients, he puts on the most dandy top-boots I ever saw, which he gets from some wonderful bootmaker a hundred miles off. His appearance is what one calls "jemmy"; there is no other word that will do for it. He was evidently a little discomfited when he saw me in my breakfast costume, with the habits which I brought with me from the fellows at Guy's; my feet against the fireplace, my chair balanced on its hind legs (a habit of sitting which I afterwards discovered he particularly abhorred); slippers on my feet (which, also, he considered a most ungentlemanly piece of untidiness "out of a bedroom"); in short, from what I afterwards learned, every prejudice he had was outraged by my appearance on this first visit of his. I put my book down, and sprang up to receive him. He stood, hat and cane in hand.

'"I came to enquire if it would be convenient for you to accompany me on my morning's round, and to be introduced to a few of our friends." I quite detected the little tone of coldness, induced by his disappointment at my appearance, though he never imagined that it was in any way perceptible. "I will be ready directly, sir," said I; and bolted into my bedroom, only too happy to escape his scrutinising eye.

'When I returned, I was made aware, by sundry indescribable little coughs and hesitating noises, that my dress did not satisfy him. I stood ready, hat and gloves in hand; but still he did not offer to set off on our round. I grew very red and hot. At length he said: "'Excuse me, my dear young friend, but may I ask if you have no other coat besides that – 'cut-away', I believe you call them? We are rather sticklers for propriety, I believe, in Duncombe; and much depends on a first impression. Let it be professional, my dear sir. Black is the garb of our profession. Forgive my speaking so plainly; but I consider myself *in loco parentis*."

'He was so kind, so bland, and, in truth, so friendly, that I felt it would be most childish to take offence; but I had a little resentment in my heart at this way of being treated. However, I murmured, "Oh, certainly, sir, if you wish it"; and returned once more to change my coat – my poor cut-away.

'"Those coats, sir, give a man rather too much of a sporting appearance, not quite befitting the learned professions; more as if you came down here to hunt than to be the Galen or Hippocrates of the neighbourhood." He smiled graciously, so I smothered a sigh; for, to tell you the truth, I had rather anticipated – and, in fact, had boasted at Guy's of – the runs I hoped to have with the hounds; for Duncombe was in a famous hunting district. But all these ideas were quite dispersed when Mr Morgan led me to the inn-yard, where there was a horse-dealer on his way to a neighbouring fair, and "strongly advised me" – which in our relative circumstances was equivalent to an injunction – to purchase a little, useful, fast-trotting, brown cob, instead of a fine showy horse, "who would take any fence I put him to", as the horse-dealer assured me. Mr Morgan was evidently pleased when I bowed to his decision, and gave up all hopes of an occasional hunt.

'He opened out a great deal more after this purchase. He told me his plan of establishing me in a house of my own, which looked more respectable, not to say professional, than being in lodgings; and then he went on to say that he had lately lost a friend, a brother surgeon in a neighbouring town, who had left a widow with a small income, who would be very glad to live with me, and act as mistress to my establishment; thus lessening the expense.

'"She is a ladylike woman," said Mr Morgan, "to judge from the little I have seen of her; about forty-five or so; and may really be of some help to you in the little etiquettes of our profession – the slight delicate attentions which every man has to learn, if he wishes to get on in life. This is Mrs Munton's, sir," said he, stopping short at a very unromantic-looking green door, with a brass knocker.

'I had no time to say, "Who is Mrs Munton?" before we had heard Mrs Munton was at home, and were following the tidy elderly servant up the narrow carpeted stairs into the drawing room. Mrs Munton was the widow of a former vicar, upwards of sixty, rather deaf, but, like all the deaf people I have ever seen, very fond of talking; perhaps because she then knew the subject, which passed out of her grasp when another began to speak. She was ill of a chronic complaint, which often incapacitated her from going out; and the kind people of the town were in the habit of coming to see her and sit with her, and of bringing her the newest, freshest titbits of news; so that her room was the centre of the gossip of Duncombe – not of scandal, mind; for I make a distinction between gossip and scandal. Now you can fancy the discrepancy between the ideal and the real Mrs Munton. Instead of any foolish notion of a beautiful blooming widow, tenderly anxious about the health of the stranger, I saw a homely, talkative, elderly person, with a keen observant eye, and marks of suffering on her face; plain in manner and dress, but still unmistakably a lady. She talked to Mr Morgan, but she looked at me; and I saw that nothing I did escaped her notice. Mr Morgan annoyed me by his anxiety to show me off, but he was kindly anxious to bring out every circumstance to my credit in Mrs Munton's hearing, knowing well that the town-crier had not more opportunities to publish all about me than she had.

"'What was that remark you repeated to me of Sir Astley Cooper's?" asked he. It had been the most trivial speech in the world that I had named as we walked along, and I felt ashamed of having to repeat it: but it answered Mr Morgan's purpose, and before night all the town had heard that I was a favourite pupil of Sir Astley's (I had never seen him but twice in my life); and Mr Morgan was afraid that as soon as he knew my full value I should be retained by Sir Astley to assist him in his duties as surgeon to the royal family. Every little circumstance was pressed into the conversation which could add to my importance.

"'As I once heard Sir Robert Peel remark to Mr Harrison, the father of our young friend here – the moons in August are remarkably full and bright." If you remember, Charles, my father was always proud of having sold a pair of gloves to Sir Robert, when he was staying at the Grange, near Biddicombe, and I suppose good Mr Morgan had paid his only visit to my father at the time; but Mrs Munton evidently looked at me with double respect after this incidental remark, which I was amused to meet with, a few months afterwards, disguised in the statement that my father was an intimate friend of the Premier's, and had, in fact, been the adviser of most of the measures taken by him in public life. I sat by, half indignant and half amused. Mr Morgan looked so complacently pleased at the whole effect of the conversation, that I did not care to mar it by explanations; and, indeed, I had little idea at the time how small sayings were the seeds of great events in the town of Duncombe. When we left Mrs Munton's, he was in a blandly communicative mood.

'"You will find it a curious statistical fact, but five-sixths of our householders of a certain rank in Duncombe are women. We have widows and old maids in rich abundance. In fact, my dear sir, I believe that you and I are almost the only gentlemen in the place – Mr Bullock, of course, excepted. By gentlemen, I mean professional men. It behoves us to remember, sir, that so many of the female sex rely upon us for the kindness and protection which every man who is worthy of the name is always so happy to render."

'Miss Tomkinson, on whom we next called, did not strike me as remarkably requiring protection from any man. She was a tall, gaunt, masculine-looking woman, with an air of defiance about her, naturally; this, however, she softened and mitigated, as far as she was able, in favour of Mr Morgan. He, it seemed to me, stood a little in awe of the lady, who was very *brusque* and plain spoken, and evidently piqued herself on her decision of character and sincerity of speech.

'"So this is the Mr Harrison we have heard so much of from you, Mr Morgan? I must say, from what I had heard, that I had expected something a little more – hum – hum! But he's young yet; he's young. We have been all anticipating an Apollo, Mr Harrison, from Mr Morgan's description, and an Aesculapius combined in one; or, perhaps I might confine myself to saying Apollo, as he, I believe, was the god of medicine!"

'How could Mr Morgan have described me without seeing me? I asked myself.

'Miss Tomkinson put on her spectacles, and adjusted them on her Roman nose. Suddenly relaxing from her severity of inspection, she said to Mr Morgan – "But you must see Caroline. I had nearly forgotten it; she is busy with the girls, but I will send for her. She had a bad headache yesterday, and looked very pale; it made me very uncomfortable."

'She rang the bell, and desired the servant to fetch Miss Caroline.

'Miss Caroline was the younger sister – younger by twenty years; and so considered as a child by Miss Tomkinson, who was fifty-five, at the very least. If she was considered as a child, she was also petted and caressed, and cared for as a child; for she had been left as a baby to the charge of her elder sister; and when the father died, and they had to set up a school, Miss Tomkinson took upon herself every difficult arrangement, and denied herself every pleasure, and made every sacrifice in order that "Carry" might not feel the change in their circumstances. My wife tells me she once knew the sisters purchase a piece of silk, enough, with management, to have made two gowns; but Carry wished for flounces, or some such fal-lals; and without a word, Miss Tomkinson gave up her gown to have the whole made up as Carry wished, into one handsome one; and wore an old shabby affair herself as cheerfully as if it were Genoa velvet. That tells the sort of relationship between the sisters as well as anything, and I consider myself very good to name it thus early; for it was long before I found out Miss Tomkinson's real goodness, and we had a great quarrel first. Miss Caroline looked very delicate and die-away when she came in; she was as soft and sentimental as Miss Tomkinson was hard and masculine; and had a way of saying, "Oh, sister, how can you?" at Miss Tomkinson's startling speeches, which I never liked – especially as it was accompanied by a sort of protesting look at the company present, as if she wished to have it understood that she was shocked at her sister's *outré* manners. Now, that was not faithful between sisters. A remonstrance in private might have done good – though, for my own part, I have grown to like Miss Tomkinson's speeches and ways; but I don't like the way some people have of separating themselves from what may be unpopular in their relations. I know I spoke rather shortly to Miss Caroline when she asked me whether I could bear the change from "the great metropolis" to a little country village. In the first place, why could not she call it "London", or "town", and have done with it? And, in the next place, why should she not love the place that was her home well enough to fancy that everyone would like it when they came to know it as well as she did?

'I was conscious I was rather abrupt in my conversation with her, and I saw that Mr Morgan was watching me, though he pretended to be listening to Miss Tomkinson's whispered account of her sister's symptoms. But when we were once more in the street, he began, "My dear young friend –"

'I winced; for all the morning I had noticed that when he was going to give a little unpalatable advice, he always began with "My dear young friend". He had done so about the horse.

'"My dear young friend, there are one or two hints I should like to give you about your manner. The great Sir Everard Home used to say, 'A general practitioner should either have a very good manner, or a very bad one.' Now, in the latter case, he must be possessed of talents and acquirements sufficient to ensure his being sought after, whatever his manner might be. But the rudeness will give notoriety to these qualifications. Abernethy is a case in point. I rather, myself, question the taste of bad manners. I, therefore, have studied to acquire an attentive, anxious politeness, which combines ease and grace with a tender regard and interest. I am not aware whether I have succeeded (few men do) in coming up to my ideal; but I recommend you to strive after this manner, peculiarly befitting our profession. Identify yourself with your patients, my dear sir. You have sympathy in your good heart, I am sure, to really feel pain when listening to their account of their sufferings, and it soothes them to see the expression of this feeling in your manner. It is, in fact, sir, manners that make the man in our profession. I don't set myself up as an example – far from it; but – this is Mr Hutton's, our Vicar; one of the servants is indisposed, and I shall be glad of the opportunity of introducing you. We can resume our conversation at another time."

'I had not been aware that we had been holding a conversation, in which, I believe, the assistance of two persons is required. Why had not Mr Hutton sent to ask after my health the evening before, according to the custom of the place? I felt rather offended.

CHAPTER III

'The vicarage was on the north side of the street, at the end opening towards the hills. It was a long low house, receding behind its neighbours; a court was between the door and the street, with a flag-walk and an old stone cistern on the right-hand side of the door; Solomon's seal growing under the windows. Someone was watching from behind the window-curtain; for the door opened, as if by magic, as soon as we reached it; and we entered a low room, which served as hall, and was matted all over, with deep old-fashioned window seats, and Dutch tiles in the fireplace; altogether it was very cool and refreshing, after the hot sun in the white and red street.

'"Bessie is not so well, Mr Morgan," said the sweet little girl of eleven or so, who had opened the door. "Sophy wanted to send for you; but papa said he was sure you would come soon this morning, and we were to remember that there were other sick people wanting you."

'"Here's Mr Morgan, Sophy," said she, opening the door into an inner room, to which we descended by a step, as I remember well; for I was nearly falling down it, I was so caught by the picture within. It was like a picture – at least, seen through the door frame. A sort of mixture of crimson and sea-green in the room, and a sunny garden beyond; a very low casement window, open to the amber air; clusters of white roses peeping in; and Sophy sitting on a cushion on the ground, the light coming from above on her head, and a little sturdy round-eyed brother kneeling by her, to whom she was teaching the alphabet. It was a mighty relief to him when we came in, as I could see; and I am much mistaken if he was easily caught again to say his lesson, when he was once sent off to find papa. Sophy rose quietly; and of course we were just introduced, and that was all, before she took Mr Morgan upstairs to see her sick servant. I was left to myself in the room. It looked so like a home that it at once made me know the full charm of the word. There were books and work about, and tokens of employment; there was a child's plaything on the floor, and against the sea-green walls there hung a likeness or two, done in watercolours; one, I am sure, was that of Sophy's mother. The chairs and sofa were covered with chintz, the same as the curtains – a little pretty red rose on a white ground. I don't know where the crimson came from, but I am sure there was crimson somewhere; perhaps in the carpet. There was a glass door besides the window, and you went up a step into the garden. This was, first, a grass plot, just under the windows, and, beyond that, straight gravel walks, with box-borders and narrow flower-beds on each side, most brilliant and gay at the end of August, as it was then; and behind the flower-borders were fruit trees trained over woodwork, so as to shut out the beds of kitchen-garden within.

'While I was looking round, a gentleman came in, who, I was sure, was the Vicar. It was rather awkward, for I had to account for my presence there.

'"I came with Mr Morgan; my name is Harrison," said I, bowing. I could see he was not much enlightened by this explanation, but we sat down and talked about the time of year, or some such matter, till Sophy and Mr Morgan came back. Then I saw Mr Morgan to advantage. With a man whom he respected, as he did the Vicar, he lost the prim, artificial manner he had in general, and was calm and dignified; but not so dignified as the Vicar. I never saw anyone like him. He was very quiet and reserved, almost absent at times; his personal appearance was not striking; but he was altogether a man you would talk to with your hat off whenever you met him. It was his character that produced this effect – character that he never thought about, but that appeared in every word, and look, and motion.

'"Sophy," said he, "Mr Morgan looks very warm; could you not gather a few jargonelle pears off the south wall? I fancy there are some ripe there. Our jargonelle pears are remarkably early this year."

'Sophy went into the sunny garden, and I saw her take a rake and tilt at the pears, which were above her reach, apparently. The parlour had become chilly (I found out afterwards it had a flag floor, which accounts for its coldness), and I thought I should like to go into the warm sun. I said I would go and help the young lady; and, without waiting for an answer, I went into the warm scented garden, where the bees were rifling the flowers, and making a continual busy sound. I think Sophy had begun to despair of getting the fruit, and was glad of my assistance. I thought I was very senseless to have knocked them down so soon, when I found we were to go in as soon as they were gathered. I should have liked to have walked round the garden, but Sophy walked straight off with the pears, and I could do nothing but follow her. She took up her needlework while we ate them: they were very soon finished, and, when the Vicar had ended his conversation with Mr Morgan about some poor people, we rose up to come away. I was thankful that Mr Morgan had said so little about me. I could not have endured that he should have introduced Sir Astley Cooper or Sir Robert Peel at the vicarage; nor yet could I have brooked much mention of my "great opportunities for acquiring a thorough knowledge of my profession", which I had heard him describe to Miss Tomkinson, while her sister was talking to me. Luckily, however, he spared me all this at the Vicar's. When we left, it was time to mount our horses and go the country rounds, and I was glad of it.

CHAPTER IV

'By and by the inhabitants of Duncombe began to have parties in my honour. Mr Morgan told me it was on my account, or I don't think I should have found it out. But he was pleased at every fresh invitation, and rubbed his hands, and chuckled, as if it was a compliment to himself, as in truth it was.

'Meanwhile, the arrangement with Mrs Rose had been brought to a conclusion. She was to bring her furniture and place it in a house, of which I was to pay the rent. She was to be the mistress, and, in return, she was not to pay anything for her board. Mr Morgan took the house and delighted in advising and settling all my affairs. I was partly indolent, and partly amused, and was altogether passive. The house he took for me was near his own: it had two sitting rooms downstairs, opening into each other by folding-doors, which were, however, kept shut in general. The back room was my consulting room ("the library", he advised me to call it), and he gave me a skull to put on the top of my bookcase, in which the medical books were all ranged on the conspicuous shelves; while Miss Austen, Dickens and Thackeray were, by Mr Morgan himself, skilfully placed in a careless way, upside down or with their backs turned to the wall. The front parlour was to be the dining room, and the room above was furnished with Mrs Rose's drawing-room chairs and table, though I found she preferred sitting downstairs in the dining room close to the window, where, between every stitch, she could look up and see what was going on in the street. I felt rather queer to be the master of this house, filled with another person's furniture, before I had even seen the lady whose property it was.

'Presently she arrived. Mr Morgan met her at the inn where the coach stopped, and accompanied her to my house. I could see them out of the drawing-room window, the little gentleman stepping daintily along, flourishing his cane, and evidently talking away. She was a little taller than he was, and in deep widow's mourning; such veils and falls, and capes and cloaks, that she looked like a black crape haycock. When we were introduced, she put up her thick veil and looked around and sighed.

'"Your appearance and circumstances, Mr Harrison, remind me forcibly of the time when I was married to my dear husband, now at rest. He was then, like you, commencing practice as a surgeon. For twenty years I sympathised with him, and assisted him by every means in my power, even to making up pills when the young man was out. May we live together in like harmony for an equal length of time! May the regard between us be equally sincere, although, instead of being conjugal, it is to be maternal and filial!"

'I am sure she had been concocting this speech in the coach, for she afterwards told me she was the only passenger. When she had ended, I felt as if I ought to have had a glass of wine in my hand to drink, after the manner of toasts. And yet I doubt if I should have done it heartily, for I did not hope to live with her for twenty years; it had rather a dreary sound. However, I only bowed and kept my thoughts to myself. I asked Mr Morgan, while Mrs Rose was upstairs taking off her things, to stay to tea; to which he agreed, and kept rubbing his hands with satisfaction, saying:

'"Very fine woman, sir; very fine woman! And what a manner! How she will receive patients, who may wish to leave a message during your absence. Such a flow of words to be sure!"

'Mr Morgan could not stay long after tea, as there were one or two cases to be seen. I would willingly have gone, and had my hat on, indeed, for the purpose, when he said it would not be respectful, "not the thing", to leave Mrs Rose the first evening of her arrival.

'"Tender deference to the sex – to a widow in the first months of her loneliness – requires a little consideration, my dear sir. I will leave that case at Miss Tomkinson's for you; you will perhaps call early tomorrow morning. Miss Tomkinson is rather particular, and is apt to speak plainly if she does not think herself properly attended to."

'I had often noticed that he shuffled off the visits to Miss Tomkinson's on me, and I suspect he was a little afraid of the lady.

'It was rather a long evening with Mrs Rose. She had nothing to do, thinking it civil, I suppose, to stop in the parlour, and not go upstairs and unpack. I begged I might be no restraint upon her if she wished to do so; but (rather to my disappointment) she smiled in a measured, subdued way, and said it would be a pleasure to her to become better acquainted with me. She went upstairs once, and my heart misgave me when I saw her come down with a clean folded pocket-handkerchief. Oh, my prophetic soul! – she was no sooner seated, than she began to give me an account of her late husband's illness, and symptoms, and death. It was a very common case, but she evidently seemed to think it had been peculiar. She had just a smattering of medical knowledge and used the technical terms so very *mal-àpropos* that I could hardly keep from smiling; but I would not have done it for the world, she was evidently in such deep and sincere distress. At last she said:

'"I have the 'dognoses' of my dear husband's complaint in my desk, Mr Harrison, if you would like to draw up the case for the *Lancet*. I think he would have felt gratified, poor fellow, if he had been told such a compliment would be paid to his remains, and that his case should appear in those distinguished columns."

'It was rather awkward; for the case was of the very commonest, as I said before. However, I had not been even this short time in practice without having learnt a few of those noises which do not compromise one, and yet may bear a very significant construction if the listener chooses to exert a little imagination.

'Before the end of the evening, we were such friends that she brought me down the late Mr Rose's picture to look at. She told me she could not bear herself to gaze upon the beloved features; but that, if I would look upon the miniature, she would avert her face. I offered to take it into my own hands, but she seemed wounded at the proposal, and said she never, never could trust such a treasure out of her own possession; so she turned her head very much over her left shoulder, while I examined the likeness held by her extended right arm.

'The late Mr Rose must have been rather a good-looking jolly man; and the artist had given him such a broad smile, and such a twinkle about the eyes, that it really was hard to help smiling back at him. However, I restrained myself.

'At first Mrs Rose objected to accepting any of the invitations which were sent her to accompany me to the tea parties in the town. She was so good and simple that I was sure she had no other reason than the one which she alleged – the short time that had elapsed since her husband's death; or else, now that I had had some experience of the entertainments which she declined so pertinaciously, I might have suspected that she was glad of the excuse. I used sometimes to wish that I was a widow. I came home tired from a hard day's riding, and, if I had but felt sure that Mr Morgan would not come in, I should certainly have put on my slippers and my loose morning coat, and have indulged in a cigar in the garden. It seemed a cruel sacrifice to society to dress myself in tight boots, and a stiff coat, and go to a five-o'clock tea. But Mr Morgan read me such lectures upon the necessity of cultivating the goodwill of the people among whom I was settled, and seemed so sorry, and almost hurt, when I once complained of the dulness of these parties, that I felt I could not be so selfish as to decline more than one out of three. Mr Morgan, if he found that I had an invitation for the evening, would often take the longer round, and the more distant visits. I suspected him at first of the design, which I confess I often entertained, of shirking the parties; but I soon found out he was really making a sacrifice of his inclinations for what he considered to be my advantage.

CHAPTER V

'There was one invitation which seemed to promise a good deal of pleasure. Mr Bullock (who is the attorney of Duncombe) was married a second time to a lady from a large provincial town; she wished to lead the fashion – a thing very easy to do, for everyone was willing to follow her. So, instead of giving a tea party in my honour, she proposed a picnic to some old hall in the neighbourhood; and really the arrangement sounded tempting enough. Every patient we had seemed full of the subject – both those who were invited and those who were not. There was a moat round the house, with a boat on it; and there was a gallery in the hall, from which music sounded delightfully. The family to whom the place belonged were abroad, and lived at a newer and grander mansion when they were at home; there were only a farmer and his wife in the old hall, and they were to have the charge of the preparations. The little kind-hearted town was delighted when the sun shone bright on the October morning of our picnic; the shopkeepers and cottagers all looked pleased as they saw the cavalcade gathering at Mr Bullock's door. We were somewhere about twenty in number; a "silent few", she called us; but I thought we were quite enough. There were the Miss Tomkinsons, and two of their young ladies – one of them belonged to a "county family", Mrs Bullock told me in a whisper; then came Mr and Mrs and Miss Bullock, and a tribe of little children, the offspring of the present wife. Miss Bullock was only a stepdaughter. Mrs Munton had accepted the invitation to join our party, which was rather unexpected by the host and hostess, I imagine, from little remarks that I overheard; but they made her very welcome. Miss Horsman (a maiden lady who had been on a visit from home till last week) was another. And last, there were the Vicar and his children. These, with Mr Morgan and myself, made up the party. I was very much pleased to see something more of the Vicar's family. He had come in occasionally to the evening parties, it is true; and spoken kindly to us all; but it was not his habit to stay very long at them. And his daughter was, he said, too young to visit. She had had the charge of her little sisters and brother since her mother's death, which took up a good deal of her time, and she was glad of the evenings to pursue her own studies. But today the case was different; and Sophy, and Helen, and Lizzie, and even little Walter, were all there, standing at Mrs Bullock's door; for we none of us could be patient enough to sit still in the parlour with Mrs Munton and the elder ones, quietly waiting for the two chaises and the spring-cart, which were to have been there by two o'clock, and now it was nearly a quarter past. "Shameful! the brightness of the day would be gone." The sympathetic shopkeepers, standing at their respective doors with their hands in their pockets, had, one and all, their heads turned in the direction from which the carriages (as Mrs Bullock called them) were to come. There was a rumble along the paved street; and the shopkeepers turned and smiled, and bowed their heads congratulatingly to us; all the mothers and all the little children of the place stood clustering round the door to see us set off. I had my horse waiting; and, meanwhile, I assisted people into their vehicles. One sees a good deal of management on such occasions. Mrs Munton was handed first into one of the chaises; then there was a little hanging back, for most of the young people wished to go in the cart – I don't know why. Miss Horsman, however, came forward, and as she was known to be the intimate friend of Mrs Munton, so far it was satisfactory. But who was to be third – bodkin with two old ladies, who liked the windows shut? I saw Sophy speaking to Helen; and then she came forward and offered to be the third. The two old ladies looked pleased and glad (as everyone did near Sophy); so that chaise-full was arranged. Just as it was going off, however, the servant from the vicarage came running with a note for her master. When he had read it, he went to the chaise door, and I suppose told Sophy, what I afterwards heard him say to Mrs Bullock, that the clergyman of a neighbouring parish was ill, and unable to read the funeral service for one of his parishioners, who was to be buried that afternoon. The Vicar was, of course, obliged to go, and said he should not return home that night. It seemed a relief to some, I perceived, to be without the little restraint of his dignified presence. Mr Morgan came up just at the moment, having ridden hard all the morning to be in time to join our party; so we were resigned, on the whole, to the Vicar's absence. His own family regretted him the most, I noticed, and I liked them all the better for it. I believe that I came next in being sorry for his departure; but I respected and admired him, and felt always the better for having been in his company. Miss Tomkinson, Mrs Bullock, and the "county" young lady were in the next chaise. I think the last would rather have been in the cart with the younger and merrier set, but I imagine that was considered *infra dig*. The remainder of the party were to ride and tie; and a most riotous laughing set they were. Mr Morgan and I were on horseback; at least I led my horse, with little Walter riding on him; his fat, sturdy legs standing stiff out on each side of my cob's broad back. He was a little darling, and chattered all the way, his sister Sophy being the heroine of all his stories. I found he owed this day's excursion entirely to her begging papa to let him come; nurse was strongly against it – "cross old nurse!" he called her once, and then said, "No, not cross; kind nurse; Sophy tells Walter not to say cross nurse." I never saw so young

29

a child so brave. The horse shied at a log of wood. Walter looked very red, and grasped the mane, but sat upright like a little man, and never spoke all the time the horse was dancing. When it was over he looked at me, and smiled:

'"You would not let me be hurt, Mr Harrison, would you?" He was the most winning little fellow I ever saw.

'There were frequent cries to me from the cart, "Oh, Mr Harrison! do get us that branch of blackberries; you can reach it with your whip handle." "Oh, Mr Harrison! there were such splendid nuts on the other side of that hedge; would you just turn back for them?" Miss Caroline Tomkinson was once or twice rather faint with the motion of the cart, and asked me for my smelling-bottle, as she had forgotten hers. I was amused at the idea of my carrying such articles about with me. Then she thought she should like to walk, and got out, and came on my side of the road; but I found little Walter the pleasanter companion, and soon set the horse off into a trot, with which pace her tender constitution could not keep up.

'The road to the old hall was along a sandy lane, with high hedge-banks; the wych-elms almost met overhead. "Shocking farming!" Mr Bullock called out; and so it might be, but it was very pleasant and picturesque-looking. The trees were gorgeous, in their orange and crimson hues, varied by great dark green holly-bushes, glistening in the autumn sun. I should have thought the colours too vivid, if I had seen them in a picture, especially when we wound up the brow, after crossing the little bridge over the brook – (what laughing and screaming there was as the cart splashed through the sparkling water!) – and I caught the purple hills beyond. We could see the old hall, too, from that point, with its warm rich woods billowing up behind, and the blue waters of the moat lying still under the sunlight.

'Laughing and talking is very hungry work, and there was a universal petition for dinner when we arrived at the lawn before the hall, where it had been arranged that we were to dine. I saw Miss Carry take Miss Tomkinson aside, and whisper to her; and presently the elder sister came up to me, where I was busy, rather apart, making a seat of hay, which I had fetched from the farmer's loft for my little friend Walter, who, I had noticed, was rather hoarse, and for whom I was afraid of a seat on the grass, dry as it appeared to be.

'"Mr Harrison, Caroline tells me she has been feeling very faint, and she is afraid of a return of one of her attacks. She says she has more confidence in your medical powers than in Mr Morgan's. I should not be sincere if I did not say that I differ from her; but, as it is so, may I beg you to keep an eye upon her? I tell her she had better not have come if she did not feel well; but, poor girl, she had set her heart upon this day's pleasure. I have offered to go home with her; but she says, if she can only feel sure you are at hand, she would rather stay."

'Of course I bowed, and promised all due attendance on Miss Caroline; and in the meantime, until she did require my services, I thought I might as well go and help the Vicar's daughter, who looked so fresh and pretty in her white muslin dress, here, there, and everywhere, now in the sunshine, now in the green shade, helping everyone to be comfortable, and thinking of everyone but herself.

'Presently Mr Morgan came up.

'"Miss Caroline does not feel quite well. I have promised your services to her sister."

'"So have I, sir. But Miss Sophy cannot carry this heavy basket."

'I did not mean her to have heard this excuse; but she caught it up and said:

'"Oh, yes, I can! I can take the things out one by one. Go to poor Miss Caroline, pray, Mr Harrison."

'I went; but very unwillingly, I must say. When I had once seated myself by her, I think she must have felt better. It was, probably, only a nervous fear, which was relieved when she knew she had assistance near at hand; for she made a capital dinner. I thought she would never end her modest requests for "just a little more pigeon-pie, or a merry-thought of chicken". Such a hearty meal would, I hope, effectually revive her; and so it did; for she told me she thought she could manage to walk round the garden, and see the old peacock yews, if I would kindly give her my arm. It was very provoking; I had so set my heart upon being with the Vicar's children. I advised Miss Caroline strongly to lie down a little, and rest before tea, on the sofa in the farmer's kitchen; you cannot think how persuasively I begged her to take care of herself. At last she consented, thanking me for my tender interest; she should never forget my kind attention to her. She little knew what was in my mind at the time. However, she was safely consigned to the farmer's wife, and I was rushing out in search of a white gown and a waving figure, when I encountered Mrs Bullock at the door of the hall. She was a fine, fierce-looking woman. I thought she had appeared a little displeased at my (unwilling) attentions to Miss Caroline at dinner time; but now, seeing me alone, she was all smiles.

'"Oh, Mr Harrison, all alone! How is that? What are the young ladies about to allow such churlishness? And, by the way, I have left a young lady who will be very glad of your assistance, I am sure – my daughter, Jemima (her stepdaughter, she meant). Mr Bullock is so particular, and so tender a father, that he would be frightened to death at the idea of her going into the boat on the moat unless she was with someone who could swim. He is gone to discuss the new wheel-plough with the farmer (you know agriculture is his hobby, although law, horrid law, is his business). But the poor girl is pining on the bank, longing for my permission to join the others, which I dare not give unless you will kindly accompany her, and promise, if any accident happens, to preserve her safe."

'Oh, Sophy, why was no one anxious about you?

CHAPTER VI

'Miss Bullock was standing by the water-side, looking wistfully, as I thought, at the water party; the sound of whose merry laughter came pleasantly enough from the boat, which lay off (for, indeed, no one knew how to row, and she was of a clumsy flat-bottomed build) about a hundred yards, "weather-bound", as they shouted out, among the long stalks of the water lilies.

'Miss Bullock did not look up till I came close to her; and then, when I told her my errand, she lifted up her great, heavy, sad eyes, and looked at me for a moment. It struck me, at the time, that she expected to find some expression on my face which was not there, and that its absence was a relief to her. She was a very pale, unhappy-looking girl, but very quiet, and, if not agreeable in manner, at any rate not forward or offensive. I called to the party in the boat, and they came slowly enough through the large, cool, green lily leaves towards us. When they got near, we saw there was no room for us, and Miss Bullock said she would rather stay in the meadow and saunter about, if I would go into the boat; and I am certain from the look on her countenance that she spoke the truth; but Miss Horsman called out, in a sharp voice, while she smiled in a very disagreeable knowing way:

'"Oh, mamma will be displeased if you don't come in, Miss Bullock, after all her trouble in making such a nice arrangement."

'At this speech the poor girl hesitated, and at last, in an undecided way, as if she was not sure whether she was doing right, she took Sophy's place in the boat. Helen and Lizzie landed with their sister, so that there was plenty of room for Miss Tomkinson, Miss Horsman, and all the little Bullocks; and the three vicarage girls went off strolling along the meadow side, and playing with Walter, who was in a high state of excitement. The sun was getting low, but the declining light was beautiful upon the water; and, to add to the charm of the time, Sophy and her sisters, standing on the green lawn in front of the hall, struck up the little German canon, which I had never heard before: "Oh, wie wohl ist mir am Abend," etc. At last we were summoned to tug the boat to the landing-steps on the lawn, tea and a blazing wood fire being ready for us in the hall. I was offering my arm to Miss Horsman, as she was a little lame, when she said again, in her peculiar disagreeable way, "Had you not better take Miss Bullock, Mr Harrison? It will be more satisfactory."

'I helped Miss Horsman up the steps, however, and then she repeated her advice; so, remembering that Miss Bullock was in fact the daughter of my entertainers, I went to her; but, though she accepted my arm, I could perceive that she was sorry that I had offered it.

'The hall was lighted by the glorious wood fire in the wide old grate; the daylight was dying away in the west; and the large windows admitted but little of what was left, through their small leaded frames, with coats of arms emblazoned upon them. The farmer's wife had set out a great long table, which was piled with good things; and a huge black kettle sang on the glowing fire, which sent a cheerful warmth through the room as it crackled and blazed. Mr Morgan (who I found had been taking a little round in the neighbourhood among his patients) was there, smiling and rubbing his hands as usual. Mr Bullock was holding a conversation with the farmer at the garden-door on the nature of different manures, in which it struck me that, if Mr Bullock had the fine names and the theories on his side, the farmer had all the practical knowledge and the experience, and I know which I would have trusted. I think Mr Bullock rather liked to talk about Liebig in my hearing; it sounded well, and was knowing. Mrs Bullock was not particularly placid in her mood. In the first place, I wanted to sit by the Vicar's daughter, and Miss Caroline as decidedly wanted to sit on my other side, being afraid of her fainting fits, I imagine. But Mrs Bullock called me to a place near her daughter. Now, I thought I had done enough civility to a girl who was evidently annoyed rather than pleased by my attentions, and I pretended to be busy stooping under the table for Miss Caroline's gloves, which were missing; but it was of no avail; Mrs Bullock's fine severe eyes were awaiting my reappearance, and she summoned me again.

'"I am keeping this place on my right hand for you, Mr Harrison. Jemima, sit still!"

'I went up to the post of honour and tried to busy myself with pouring out coffee to hide my chagrin; but, on my forgetting to empty the water put in ("to warm the cups", Mrs Bullock said), and omitting to add any sugar, the lady told me she would dispense with my services, and turn me over to my neighbour on the other side.

'"Talking to the younger lady was, no doubt, more Mr Harrison's vocation than assisting the elder one." I dare say it was only the manner that made the words seem offensive. Miss Horsman sat opposite to me, smiling away, Miss Bullock did not speak, but seemed more depressed than ever. At length, Miss Horsman and Mrs Bullock got to a war of innuendoes, which were completely unintelligible to me, and I was very much displeased with my situation; while, at the bottom of the table, Mr Morgan and Mr Bullock were making the young ones laugh most heartily. Part of the joke was Mr Morgan insisting upon making tea at the end; and Sophy and Helen were busy contriving every possible mistake for him. I thought honour was a very good thing, but merriment a better. Here was I in the place of distinction, hearing nothing but cross words. At last the time came for us to go home. As the evening was damp, the seats in the chaises were the best and most to be desired. And now Sophy offered to go in the cart; only she seemed anxious, and so was I, that Walter should be secured from the effects of the white wreaths of fog rolling up from the valley; but the little violent, affectionate fellow would not be separated from Sophy. She made a nest for him on her knee in one corner of the cart, and covered him with her own shawl; and I hoped that he would take no harm. Miss Tomkinson, Mr Bullock, and some of the young ones walked; but I seemed chained to the windows of the chaise, for Miss Caroline begged me not to leave her, as she was dreadfully afraid of robbers; and Mrs Bullock implored me to see that the man did not overturn them in the bad roads, as he had certainly had too much to drink.

'I became so irritable before I reached home, that I thought it was the most disagreeable day of pleasure I had ever had, and could hardly bear to answer Mrs Rose's never-ending questions. She told me, however, that from my account the day was so charming that she thought she should relax in the rigour of her seclusion, and mingle a little more in the society of which I gave so tempting a description. She really thought her dear Mr Rose would have wished it; and his will should be law to her after his death, as it had ever been during his life. In compliance, there-fore, with his wishes, she would even do a little violence to her own feelings.

'She was very good and kind; not merely attentive to everything which she thought could conduce to my comfort, but willing to take any trouble in providing the broths and nourishing food which I often found it convenient to order, under the name of kitchen-physic, for my poorer patients; and I really did not see the use of her shutting herself up, in mere compliance with an etiquette, when she began to wish to mix in the little quiet society of Duncombe. Accordingly I urged her to begin to visit, and, even when applied to as to what I imagined the late Mr Rose's wishes on that subject would have been, answered for that worthy gentleman, and assured his widow that I was convinced he would have regretted deeply her giving way to immoderate grief, and would have been rather grateful than otherwise at seeing her endeavour to divert her thoughts by a few quiet visits. She cheered up, and said, "As I really thought so, she would sacrifice her own inclinations, and accept the very next invitation that came."

CHAPTER VII

'I was roused from my sleep in the middle of the night by a messenger from the vicarage. Little Walter had got the croup, and Mr Morgan had been sent for into the country. I dressed myself hastily, and went through the quiet little street. There was a light burning upstairs at the vicarage. It was in the nursery. The servant, who opened the door the instant I knocked, was crying sadly, and could hardly answer my enquiries as I went upstairs, two steps at a time, to see my little favourite.

'The nursery was a great large room. At the farther end it was lighted by a common candle, which left the other end, where the door was, in shade; so I suppose the nurse did not see me come in, for she was speaking very crossly.

'"Miss Sophy!" said she, "I told you over and over again it was not fit for him to go, with the hoarseness that he had; and you would take him. It will break your papa's heart, I know; but it's none of my doing."

'Whatever Sophy felt, she did not speak in answer to this. She was on her knees by the warm bath, in which the little fellow was struggling to get his breath, with a look of terror on his face that I have often noticed in young children when smitten by a sudden and violent illness. It seems as if they recognised something infinite and invisible, at whose bidding the pain and the anguish come, from which no love can shield them. It is a very heart-rending look to observe, because it comes on the faces of those who are too young to receive comfort from the words of faith, or the promises of religion. Walter had his arms tight round Sophy's neck, as if she, hitherto his paradise-angel, could save him from the grave shadow of Death. Yes! of Death! I knelt down by him on the other side, and examined him. The very robustness of his little frame gave violence to the disease, which is always one of the most fearful by which children of his age can be attacked.

'"Don't tremble, Watty," said Sophy, in a soothing tone; "it's Mr Harrison, darling, who let you ride on his horse." I could detect the quivering in the voice, which she tried to make so calm and soft to quiet the little fellow's fears. We took him out of the bath, and I went for leeches. While I was away, Mr Morgan came. He loved the vicarage children as if he were their uncle; but he stood still and aghast at the sight of Walter – so lately bright and strong – and now hurrying along to the awful change – to the silent mysterious land, where, tended and cared for as he had been on earth, he must go – alone. The little fellow! the darling!

'We applied the leeches to his throat. He resisted at first; but Sophy, God bless her! put the agony of her grief on one side, and thought only of him, and began to sing the little songs he loved. We were all still. The gardener had gone to fetch the Vicar; but he was twelve miles off and we doubted if he would come in time. I don't know if they had any hope; but, the first moment Mr Morgan's eyes met mine, I saw that he, like me, had none. The ticking of the house clock sounded through the dark quiet house. Walter was sleeping now, with the black leeches yet hanging to his fair, white throat. Still Sophy went on singing little lullabies, which she had sung under far different and happier circumstances. I remember one verse, because it struck me at the time as strangely applicable.

> *Sleep, baby, sleep!*
> *Thy rest shall angels keep;*
> *While on the grass the lamb shall feed,*
> *And never suffer want or need,*
> *Sleep, baby, sleep.*

'The tears were in Mr Morgan's eyes. I do not think either he or I could have spoken in our natural tones; but the brave girl went on clear though low. She stopped at last, and looked up.

'"He is better, is he not, Mr Morgan?"

'"No, my dear. He is – ahem" – he could not speak all at once. Then he said – "My dear! he will be better soon. Think of your mamma, my dear Miss Sophy. She will be very thankful to have one of her darlings safe with her, where she is."

'Still she did not cry. But she bent her head down on the little face, and kissed it long and tenderly.

'"I will go for Helen and Lizzie. They will be sorry not to see him again." She rose up and went for them. Poor girls, they came in, in their dressing gowns, with eyes dilated with sudden emotion, pale with terror, stealing softly along, as if sound could disturb him. Sophy comforted them by gentle caresses. It was over soon.

'Mr Morgan was fairly crying like a child. But he thought it necessary to apologise to me, for what I honoured him for. "I am a little overdone by yesterday's work, sir. I have had one or two bad nights, and they rather upset me. When I was your age I was as strong and manly as anyone, and would have scorned to shed tears."

'Sophy came up to where we stood.

'"Mr Morgan! I am so sorry for papa. How shall I tell him?" She was struggling against her own grief for her father's sake. Mr Morgan offered to await his coming home; and she seemed thankful for the proposal. I, new friend, almost a stranger, might stay no longer. The street was as quiet as ever; not a shadow was changed; for it was not yet four o'clock. But during the night a soul had departed.

'From all I could see, and all I could learn, the Vicar and his daughter strove which should comfort the other the most. Each thought of the other's grief – each prayed for the other rather than for themselves. We saw them walking out, countrywards; and we heard of them in the cottages of the poor. But it was some time before I happened to meet either of them again. And then I felt, from something indescribable in their manner towards me, that I was one of the "Peculiar people, whom Death had made dear".

'That one day at the old hall had done this. I was, perhaps, the last person who had given the poor little fellow any unusual pleasure. Poor Walter! I wish I could have done more to make his short life happy!

CHAPTER VIII

'There was a little lull, out of respect to the Vicar's grief, in the visiting. It gave time to Mrs Rose to soften down the anguish of her weeds.

'At Christmas, Miss Tomkinson sent out invitations for a party. Miss Caroline had once or twice apologised to me because such an event had not taken place before; but, as she said, "the avocations of their daily life prevented their having such little *réunions* except in the vacations." And, sure enough, as soon as the holidays began, came the civil little note:

'"The Misses Tomkinson request the pleasure of Mrs Rose's and Mr Harrison's company at tea, on the evening of Monday, the 23rd inst. Tea at five o'clock."

'Mrs Rose's spirit roused, like a warhorse at the sound of the trumpet, at this. She was not of a repining disposition, but I do think she believed the party-giving population of Duncombe had given up inviting her, as soon as she had determined to relent, and accept the invitations, in compliance with the late Mr Rose's wishes.

'Such snippings of white love-ribbon as I found everywhere, making the carpet untidy! One day, too unluckily, a small box was brought to me by mistake. I did not look at the direction, for I never doubted it was some hyoscyamus which I was expecting from London; so I tore it open, and saw inside a piece of paper, with "No more grey hair", in large letters, upon it. I folded it up in a hurry, and sealed it afresh, and gave it to Mrs Rose; but I could not refrain from asking her, soon after, if she could recommend me anything to keep my hair from turning grey, adding that I thought prevention was better than cure. I think she made out the impression of my seal on the paper after that; for I learned that she had been crying, and that she talked about there being no sympathy left in the world for her since Mr Rose's death; and that she counted the days until she could rejoin him in the better world. I think she counted the days to Miss Tomkinson's party, too; she talked so much about it.

'The covers were taken off Miss Tomkinson's chairs, and curtains, and sofas; and a great jar full of artificial flowers was placed in the centre of the table, which, as Miss Caroline told me, was all her doing, as she doted on the beautiful and artistic in life. Miss Tomkinson stood, erect as a grenadier, close to the door, receiving her friends, and heartily shaking them by the hands as they entered; she said she was truly glad to see them. And so she really was.

'We had just finished tea, and Miss Caroline had brought out a little pack of conversation cards – sheaves of slips of cardboard, with intellectual or sentimental questions on one set, and equally intellectual and sentimental answers on the other; and, as the answers were fit to any and all the questions, you may think they were a characterless and "wersh" set of things. I had just been asked by Miss Caroline:

'"*Can you tell what those dearest to you think of you at this present time?*" and had answered: "*How can you expect me to reveal such a secret to the present company!*" when the servant announced that a gentleman, a friend of mine, wished to speak to me downstairs.

'"Oh, show him up, Martha; show him up!" said Miss Tomkinson, in her hospitality.

'"Any friend of our friend is welcome," said Miss Caroline, in an insinuating tone.

'I jumped up, however, thinking it might be someone on business; but I was so penned in by the spider-legged tables, stuck out on every side, that I could not make the haste I wished; and, before I could prevent it, Martha had shown up Jack Marshland, who was on his road home for a day or two at Christmas.

'He came up in a hearty way, bowing to Miss Tomkinson, and explaining that he had found himself in my neighbourhood, and had come over to pass a night with me, and that my servant had directed him where I was.

'His voice, loud at all times, sounded like Stentor's in that little room, where we all spoke in a kind of purring way. He had no swell in his tones; they were *forte* from the beginning. At first it seemed like the days of my youth come back again, to hear full manly speaking; I felt proud of my friend, as he thanked Miss Tomkinson for her kindness in asking him to stay the evening. By and by he came up to me, and I dare say he thought he had lowered his voice, for he looked as if speaking confidentially, while in fact the whole room might have heard him.

'"Frank, my boy, when shall we have dinner at this good old lady's? I'm deuced hungry."

'"Dinner! Why, we had had tea an hour ago." While he yet spoke, Martha came in with a little tray on which was a single cup of coffee and three slices of wafer bread-and-butter. His dismay, and his evident submission to the decrees of Fate, tickled me so much, that I thought he should have a further taste of the life I led from month's end to month's end, and I gave up my plan of taking him home at once, and enjoyed the anticipation of the hearty laugh we should have together at the end of the evening. I was famously punished for my determination.

'"Shall we continue our game?" asked Miss Caroline, who had never relinquished her sheaf of questions.

'We went on questioning and answering, with little gain of information to either party.

'"No such thing as heavy betting in this game, eh, Frank?" asked Jack, who had been watching us. "You don't lose ten pounds at a sitting, I guess, as you used to do at Short's. Playing for love, I suppose you call it?"

'Miss Caroline simpered, and looked down. Jack was not thinking of her. He was thinking of the days we had had "at the Mermaid". Suddenly he said, "Where were you this day last year, Frank?"

'"I don't remember!" said I.

'"Then I'll tell you. It's the 23rd – the day you were taken up for knocking down the fellow in Long Acre, and that I had to bail you out ready for Christmas Day. You are in more agreeable quarters tonight."

'He did not intend this reminiscence to be heard, but was not in the least put out when Miss Tomkinson, with a face of dire surprise, asked:

'"Mr Harrison taken up, sir?"

'"Oh, yes, ma'am; and you see it was so common an affair with him to be locked up that he can't remember the dates of his different imprisonments."

'He laughed heartily; and so should I have done, but that I saw the impression it made. The thing was, in fact, simple enough, and capable of easy explanation. I had been made angry by seeing a great hulking fellow, out of mere wantonness, break the crutch from under a cripple; and I struck the man more violently than I intended, and down he went, yelling out for the police, and I had to go before the magistrate to be released. I disdained giving this explanation at the time. It was no business of theirs what I had been doing a year ago; but still Jack might have held his tongue. However, that unruly member of his was set a-going, and he told me afterwards he was resolved to let the old ladies into a little of life; and accordingly he remembered every practical joke we had ever had, and talked and laughed, and roared again. I tried to converse with Miss Caroline – Mrs Munton – anyone; but Jack was the hero of the evening, and everyone was listening to him.

'"Then he has never sent any hoaxing letters since he came here, has he? Good boy! He has turned over a new leaf. He was the deepest dog at that I ever met with. Such anonymous letters as he used to send! Do you remember that to Mrs Walbrook, eh, Frank? That was too bad!" (the wretch was laughing all the time). "No; I won't tell about it – don't be afraid. Such a shameful hoax!" (laughing again).

'"Pray do tell," I called out; for it made it seem far worse than it was.

'"Oh no, no; you've established a better character – I would not for the world nip your budding efforts. We'll bury the past in oblivion."

'I tried to tell my neighbours the story to which he alluded; but they were attracted by the merriment of Jack's manner, and did not care to hear the plain matter of fact.

'Then came a pause; Jack was talking almost quietly to Miss Horsman. Suddenly he called across the room – "How many times have you been out with the hounds? The hedges were blind very late this year, but you have had some good mild days since."

'"I have never been out," said I shortly.

'"Never! – whew! – Why, I thought that was the great attraction to Duncombe."

'Now was not he provoking! He would condole with me, and fix the subject in the minds of everyone present.

'The supper trays were brought in, and there was a shuffling of situations. He and I were close together again.

'"I say, Frank, what will you lay me that I don't clear that tray before people are ready for their second helping? I'm as hungry as a hound."

'"You shall have a round of beef and a raw leg of mutton when you get home. Only do behave yourself here."

'"Well, for your sake; but keep me away from those trays, or I'll not answer for myself. 'Hould me, or I'll fight', as the Irishman said. I'll go and talk to that little old lady in blue, and sit with my back to those ghosts of eatables."

'He sat down by Miss Caroline, who would not have liked his description of her; and began an earnest, tolerably quiet conversation. I tried to be as agreeable as I could, to do away with the impression he had given of me; but I found that everyone drew up a little stiffly at my approach, and did not encourage me to make any remarks.

'In the middle of my attempts, I heard Miss Caroline beg Jack to take a glass of wine, and I saw him help himself to what appeared to be port; but in an instant he set it down from his lips, exclaiming, "Vinegar, by Jove!" He made the most horribly wry face: and Miss Tomkinson came up in a severe hurry to investigate the affair. It turned out it was some blackcurrant wine, on which she particularly piqued herself; I drank two glasses of it to ingratiate myself with her, and can testify to its sourness. I don't think she noticed my exertions, she was so much engrossed in listening to Jack's excuses for his *mal-àpropos* observation. He told her, with the gravest face, that he had been a teetotaller so long that he had but a confused recollection of the distinction between wine and vinegar, particularly eschewing the latter, because it had been twice fermented; and that he had imagined Miss Caroline had asked him to take toast-and-water, or he should never have touched the decanter.

CHAPTER IX

'As we were walking home, Jack said, "Lord, Frank! I've had such fun with the little lady in blue. I told her you wrote to me every Saturday, telling me the events of the week. She took it all in." He stopped to laugh; for he bubbled and chuckled so that he could not laugh and walk. "And I told her you were deeply in love" (another laugh); "and that I could not get you to tell me the name of the lady, but that she had light brown hair – in short, I drew from life, and gave her an exact description of herself; and that I was most anxious to see her, and implore her to be merciful to you, for that you were a most timid, faint-hearted fellow with women." He laughed till I thought he would have fallen down. "I begged her, if she could guess who it was from my description – I'll answer for it she did – I took care of that; for I said you described a mole on the left cheek, in the most poetical way, saying Venus had pinched it out of envy at seeing anyone more lovely – oh, hold me up, or I shall fall – laughing and hunger make me so weak; – well, I say, I begged her, if she knew who your fair one could be, to implore her to save you. I said I knew one of your lungs had gone after a former love affair, and that I could not answer for the other if the lady here were cruel. She spoke of a respirator; but I told her that might do very well for the odd lung; but would it minister to a heart diseased? I really did talk fine. I have found out the secret of eloquence – it's believing what you've got to say; and I worked myself well up with fancying you married to the little lady in blue."

'I got to laughing at last, angry as I had been; his impudence was irresistible. Mrs Rose had come home in the sedan, and gone to bed; and he and I sat up over the round of beef and brandy-and-water till two o'clock in the morning.

'He told me I had got quite into the professional way of mousing about a room, and mewing and purring according as my patients were ill or well. He mimicked me, and made me laugh at myself. He left early the next morning.

'Mr Morgan came at his usual hour; he and Marshland would never have agreed, and I should have been uncomfortable to see two friends of mine disliking and despising each other.

'Mr Morgan was ruffled; but with his deferential manner to women, he smoothed himself down before Mrs Rose – regretted that he had not been able to come to Miss Tomkinson's the evening before, and consequently had not seen her in the society she was so well calculated to adorn. But when we were by ourselves, he said:

'"I was sent for to Mrs Munton's this morning – the old spasms. May I ask what is this story she tells me about – about prison, in fact? I trust, sir, she has made some little mistake, and that you never were – that it is an unfounded report." He could not get it out – "that you were in Newgate for three months!" I burst out laughing; the story had grown like a mushroom indeed. Mr Morgan looked grave. I told him the truth. Still he looked grave. "I've no doubt, sir, that you acted rightly; but it has an awkward sound. I imagined from your hilarity just now that there was no foundation whatever for the story. Unfortunately, there is."

'"I was only a night at the police station. I would go there again for the same cause, sir."

'"Very fine spirit, sir – quite like Don Quixote, but don't you see you might as well have been to the hulks at once?"

'"No, sir; I don't."

'"Take my word, before long, the story will have grown to that. However, we won't anticipate evil. *Mens conscia recti*, you remember, is the great thing. The part I regret is, that it may require some short time to overcome a little prejudice which the story may excite against you. However, we won't dwell on it. *Mens conscia recti*! Don't think about it, sir."

'It was clear he was thinking a good deal about it.

CHAPTER X

'Two or three days before this time, I had had an invitation from the Bullocks to dine with them on Christmas Day. Mrs Rose was going to spend the week with friends in the town where she formerly lived; and I had been pleased at the notion of being received into a family, and of being a little with Mr Bullock, who struck me as a bluff, good-hearted fellow.

'But this Tuesday before Christmas Day, there came an invitation from the Vicar to dine there; there were to be only their own family and Mr Morgan. "Only their own family". It was getting to be all the world to me. I was in a passion with myself for having been so ready to accept Mr Bullock's invitation – coarse and ungentlemanly as he was; with his wife's airs of pretension and Miss Bullock's stupidity. I turned it over in my mind. No! I could not have a bad headache, which should prevent me going to the place I did not care for, and yet leave me at liberty to go where I wished. All I could do was to join the vicarage girls after church, and walk by their side in a long country ramble. They were quiet; not sad, exactly; but it was evident that the thought of Walter was in their minds on this day. We went through a copse where there were a good number of evergreens planted as covers for game. The snow was on the ground; but the sky was clear and bright, and the sun glittered on the smooth holly leaves. Lizzie asked me to gather her some of the very bright red berries, and she was beginning a sentence with:

'"Do you remember" – when Helen said, "Hush," and looked towards Sophy, who was walking a little apart, and crying softly to herself. There was evidently some connection between Walter and the holly berries, for Lizzie threw them away at once when she saw Sophy's tears. Soon we came to a stile which led to an open breezy common, half covered with gorse. I helped the little girls over it, and set them to run down the slope; but took Sophy's arm in mine, and, though I could not speak, I think she knew how I was feeling for her. I could hardly bear to bid her goodbye at the vicarage gate; it seemed as if I ought to go in and spend the day with her.

CHAPTER XI

'I vented my ill humour in being late for the Bullocks' dinner. There were one or two clerks, towards whom Mr Bullock was patronising and pressing. Mrs Bullock was decked out in extraordinary finery. Miss Bullock looked plainer than ever; but she had on some old gown or other, I think, for I heard Mrs Bullock tell her she was always making a figure of herself. I began today to suspect that the mother would not be sorry if I took a fancy to the stepdaughter. I was again placed near her at dinner, and, when the little ones came in to dessert, I was made to notice how fond of children she was – and, indeed, when one of them nestled to her, her face did brighten; but, the moment she caught this loud-whispered remark, the gloom came back again, with something even of anger in her look; and she was quite sullen and obstinate when urged to sing in the drawing room. Mrs Bullock turned to me:

'"Some young ladies won't sing unless they are asked by gentlemen." She spoke very crossly. "If you ask Jemima, she will probably sing. To oblige me, it is evident she will not."

'I thought the singing, when we got it, would probably be a great bore; however, I did as I was bid, and went with my request to the young lady, who was sitting a little apart. She looked up at me with eyes full of tears, and said, in a decided tone (which, if I had not seen her eyes, I should have said was as cross as her mamma's), "No, sir, I will not." She got up, and left the room. I expected to hear Mrs Bullock abuse her for her obstinacy. Instead of that, she began to tell me of the money that had been spent on her education; of what each separate accomplishment had cost. "She was timid," she said, "but very musical. Wherever her future home might be, there would be no want of music." She went on praising her till I hated her. If they thought I was going to marry that great lubberly girl, they were mistaken. Mr Bullock and the clerks came up. He brought out Liebig, and called me to him.

"'I can understand a good deal of this agricultural chemistry," said he, "and have put it in practice – without much success, hitherto, I confess. But these unconnected letters puzzle me a little. I suppose they have some meaning, or else I should say it was mere book-making to put them in."

"'I think they give the page a very ragged appearance," said Mrs Bullock, who had joined us. "I inherit a little of my late father's taste for books, and must say I like to see a good type, a broad margin, and all elegant binding. My father despised variety; how he could have held up his hands aghast at the cheap literature of these times! He did not require many books, but he would have twenty editions of those that he had; and he paid more for binding than he did for the books themselves. But elegance was everything with him. He would not have admitted your Liebig, Mr Bullock; neither the nature of the subject, nor the common type, nor the common way in which your book is got up, would have suited him."

"'Go and make tea, my dear and leave Mr Harrison and me to talk over a few of these manures."

'We settled to it; I explained the meaning of the symbols, and the doctrine of chemical equivalents. At last he said, "Doctor! you're giving me too strong a dose of it at one time. Let's have a small quantity taken 'hodie'; that's professional, as Mr Morgan would call it. Come in and call, when you have leisure, and give me a lesson in my alphabet. Of all you've been telling me I can only remember that C means carbon and O oxygen; and I see one must know the meaning of all these confounded letters before one can do much good with Liebig."

'"We dine at three," said Mrs Bullock. "There will always be a knife and fork for Mr Harrison. Bullock! don't confine your invitation to the evening."

'"Why, you see, I've a nap always after dinner; so I could not be learning chemistry then."

'"Don't be selfish, Mr B. Think of the pleasure Jemima and I shall have in Mr Harrison's society."

'I put a stop to the discussion by saying I would come in in the evenings occasionally, and give Mr Bullock a lesson, but that my professional duties occupied me invariably until that time.

'I liked Mr Bullock. He was simple and shrewd; and to be with a man was a relief, after all the feminine society I went through every day.

CHAPTER XII

'The next morning I met Miss Horsman.

'"So you dined at Mr Bullock's yesterday, Mr Harrison? Quite a family party, I hear. They are quite charmed with you, and your knowledge of chemistry. Mr Bullock told me so, in Hodgson's shop, just now. Miss Bullock is a nice girl, eh, Mr Harrison?" She looked sharply at me. Of course, whatever I thought, I could do nothing but assent. "A nice little fortune, too – three thousand pounds, Consols, from her own mother."

'What did I care? She might have three millions for me. I had begun to think a good deal about money, though, but not in connection with her. I had been doing up our books ready to send out our Christmas bills, and had been wondering how far the Vicar would consider three hundred a year, with a prospect of increase, would justify me in thinking of Sophy. Think of her I could not help; and, the more I thought of how good, and sweet, and pretty she was, the more I felt that she ought to have far more than I could offer. Besides, my father was a shopkeeper, and I saw the Vicar had a sort of respect for family. I determined to try and be very attentive to my profession. I was as civil as could be to everyone; and wore the nap off the brim of my hat by taking it off so often.

'I had my eyes open to every glimpse of Sophy. I am over-stocked with gloves now that I bought at that time, by way of making errands into the shops where I saw her black gown. I bought pounds upon pounds of arrowroot, till I was tired of the eternal arrowroot puddings Mrs Rose gave me. I asked her if she could not make bread of it, but she seemed to think that would be expensive; so I took to soap as a safe purchase. I believe soap improves by keeping.

CHAPTER XIII

'The more I knew of Mrs Rose, the better I liked her. She was sweet, and kind, and motherly, and we never had any rubs. I hurt her once or twice, I think, by cutting her short in her long stories about Mr Rose. But I found out that when she had plenty to do she did not think of him quite so much; so I expressed a wish for Corazza shirts, and, in the puzzle of devising how they were to be cut out, she forgot Mr Rose for some time. I was still more pleased by her way about some legacy her elder brother left her. I don't know the amount, but it was something handsome, and she might have set up housekeeping for herself; but, instead, she told Mr Morgan (who repeated it to me), that she should continue with me, as she had quite an elder sister's interest in me.

'The "county young lady", Miss Tyrrell, returned to Miss Tomkinson's after the holidays. She had an enlargement of the tonsils, which required to be frequently touched with caustic, so I often called to see her. Miss Caroline always received me, and kept me talking in her washed-out style, after I had seen my patient. One day she told me she thought she had a weakness about the heart, and would be glad if I would bring my stethoscope the next time, which I accordingly did! and, while I was on my knees listening to the pulsations, one of the young ladies came in. She said: "Oh dear! I never! I beg your pardon, ma'am," and scuttled out. There was not much the matter with Miss Caroline's heart: a little feeble in action or so, a mere matter of weakness and general languor. When I went down I saw two or three of the girls peeping out of the half-closed schoolroom door, but they shut it immediately, and I heard them laughing. The next time I called, Miss Tomkinson was sitting in state to receive me.

'"Miss Tyrrell's throat does not seem to make much progress. Do you understand the case, Mr Harrison, or should we have further advice? I think Mr Morgan would probably know more about it."

'I assured her that it was the simplest thing in the world; that it always implied a little torpor in the constitution, and that we preferred working through the system, which of course was a slow process; and that the medicine the young lady was taking (iodide of iron) was sure to be successful, although the progress would not be rapid. She bent her head, and said, "It might be so; but she confessed she had more confidence in medicines which had some effect."

'She seemed to expect me to tell her something; but I had nothing to say, and accordingly I bade goodbye. Somehow, Miss Tomkinson always managed to make me feel very small, by a succession of snubbings; and, whenever I left her I had always to comfort myself under her contradictions by saying to myself, "Her saying it is so does not make it so." Or I invented good retorts which I might have made to her brusque speeches, if I had but thought of them at the right time. But it was provoking that I had not had the presence of mind to recollect them just when they were wanted.

CHAPTER XIV

'On the whole, things went on smoothly. Mr Holden's legacy came in just about this time; and I felt quite rich. Five hundred pounds would furnish the house, I thought, when Mrs Rose left and Sophy came. I was delighted, too, to imagine that Sophy perceived the difference of my manner to her from what it was to anyone else, and that she was embarrassed and shy in consequence, but not displeased with me for it. All was so flourishing that I went about on wings instead of feet. We were very busy, without having anxious cares. My legacy was paid into Mr Bullock's hands, who united a little banking business to his profession of law. In return for his advice about investments (which I never meant to take, having a more charming, if less profitable, mode in my head), I went pretty frequently to teach him his agricultural chemistry. I was so happy in Sophy's blushes that I was universally benevolent, and desirous of giving pleasure to everyone. I went, at Mrs Bullock's general invitation, to dinner there one day unexpectedly: but there was such a fuss of ill-concealed preparation consequent upon my coming, that I never went again. Her little boy came in, with an audibly given message from cook, to ask: "If this was the gentleman as she was to send in the best dinner-service and dessert for?"

'I looked deaf, but determined never to go again.

'Miss Bullock and I, meanwhile, became rather friendly. We found out that we mutually disliked each other, and were contented with the discovery. If people are worth anything, this sort of non-liking is a very good beginning of friendship. Every good quality is revealed naturally and slowly, and is a pleasant surprise. I found out that Miss Bullock was sensible, and even sweet-tempered, when not irritated by her stepmother's endeavours to show her off. But she would sulk for hours after Mrs Bullock's offensive praise of her good points. And I never saw such a black passion as she went into, when she suddenly came into the room when Mrs Bullock was telling me of all the offers she had had.

'My legacy made me feel up to extravagance. I scoured the country for a glorious nosegay of camellias, which I sent to Sophy on Valentine's Day. I durst not add a line; but I wished the flowers could speak, and tell her how I loved her.

'I called on Miss Tyrrell that day. Miss Caroline was more simpering and affected than ever, and full of allusions to the day.

'"Do you affix much sincerity of meaning to the little gallantries of this day, Mr Harrison?" asked she, in a languishing tone. I thought of my camellias, and how my heart had gone with them into Sophy's keeping; and I told her I thought one might often take advantage of such a time to hint at feelings one dared not fully express.

'I remembered afterwards the forced display she made, after Miss Tyrrell left the room, of a valentine. But I took no notice at the time; my head was full of Sophy.

'It was on that very day that John Brouncker, the gardener to all of us who had small gardens to keep in order, fell down and injured his wrist severely (I don't give you the details of the case, because they would not interest you, being too technical; if you've any curiosity, you will find them in the *Lancet* of August in that year). We all liked John, and this accident was felt like a town's misfortune. The gardens, too, just wanted doing up. Both Mr Morgan and I went directly to him. It was a very awkward case, and his wife and children were crying sadly. He himself was in great distress at being thrown out of work. He begged us to do something that would cure him speedily, as he could not afford to be laid up, with six children depending on him for bread. We did not say much before him; but we both thought the arm would have to come off, and it was his right arm. We talked it over when we came out of the cottage. Mr Morgan had no doubt of the necessity. I went back at dinnertime to see the poor fellow. He was feverish and anxious. He had caught up some expression of Mr Morgan's in the morning, and had guessed the measure we had in contemplation. He bade his wife leave the room, and spoke to me by myself.

'"If you please, sir, I'd rather be done for at once than have my arm taken off, and be a burden to my family. I'm not afraid of dying; but I could not stand being a cripple for life, eating bread, and not able to earn it."

'The tears were in his eyes with earnestness. I had all along been more doubtful about the necessity of the amputation than Mr Morgan. I knew the improved treatment in such cases. In his days there was much more of the rough and ready in surgical practice; so I gave the poor fellow some hope.

'In the afternoon I met Mr Bullock.

'"So you're to try your hand at an amputation tomorrow, I hear. Poor John Brouncker! I used to tell him he was not careful enough about his ladders. Mr Morgan is quite excited about it. He asked me to be present, and see how well a man from Guy's could operate; he says he is sure you'll do it beautifully. Pah! no such sights for me, thank you."

'Ruddy Mr Bullock went a shade or two paler at the thought.

'"Curious, how professionally a man views these things! Here's Mr Morgan, who had been all along as proud of you as if you were his own son, absolutely rubbing his hands at the idea of this crowning glory, this feather in your cap! He told me just now he knew he had always been too nervous to be a good operator, and had therefore preferred sending for White from Chesterton. But now anyone might have a serious accident who liked, for you would be always at hand."

'I told Mr Bullock, I really thought we might avoid the amputation; but his mind was preoccupied with the idea of it, and he did not care to listen to me. The whole town was full of it. That is a charm in a little town, everybody is so sympathetically full of the same events. Even Miss Horsman stopped me to ask after John Brouncker with interest; but she threw cold water upon my intention of saving the arm.

"'As for the wife and family, we'll take care of them. Think what a fine opportunity you have of showing off, Mr Harrison!"

'That was just like her. Always ready with her suggestions of ill-natured or interested motives.

'Mr Morgan heard my proposal of a mode of treatment by which I thought it possible that the arm might be saved.

"'I differ from you, Mr Harrison," said he. "I regret it; but I differ *in toto* from you. Your kind heart deceives you in this instance. There is no doubt that amputation must take place – not later than tomorrow morning, I should say. I have made myself at liberty to attend upon you, sir; I shall be happy to officiate as your assistant. Time was when I should have been proud to be principal; but a little trembling in my arm incapacitates me."

'I urged my reasons upon him again; but he was obstinate. He had, in fact, boasted so much of my acquirements as an operator that he was unwilling I should lose this opportunity of displaying my skill. He could not see that there would be greater skill evinced in saving the arm; nor did I think of this at the time. I grew angry at his old-fashioned narrow-mindedness, as I thought it; and I became dogged in my resolution to adhere to my own course. We parted very coolly; and I went straight off to

John Brouncker to tell him I believed that I could save the arm, if he would refuse to have it amputated. When I calmed myself a little, before going in and speaking to him, I could not help acknowledging that we should run some risk of lockjaw; but, on the whole, and after giving some earnest conscientious thought to the case, I was sure that my mode of treatment would be best.

'He was a sensible man. I told him the difference of opinion that existed between Mr Morgan and myself. I said that there might be some little risk attending the non-amputation, but that I should guard against it; and I trusted that I should be able to preserve his arm.

'"Under God's blessing," said he reverently. I bowed my head. I don't like to talk too frequently of the dependence which I always felt on that holy blessing, as to the result of my efforts; but I was glad to hear that speech of John's, because it showed a calm and faithful heart; and I had almost certain hopes of him from that time.

'We agreed that he should tell Mr Morgan the reason of his objections to the amputation, and his reliance on my opinion. I determined to recur to every book I had relating to such case, and to convince Mr Morgan, if I could, of my wisdom. Unluckily, I found out afterwards that he had met Miss Horsman in the time that intervened before I saw him again at his own house that evening; and she had more than hinted that I shrunk from performing the operation, "for very good reasons no doubt. She had heard that the medical students in London were a bad set, and were not remarkable for regular attendance in the hospitals. She might be mistaken; but she thought it was, perhaps, quite as well poor John Brouncker had not his arm cut off by – Was there not such a thing as mortification coming on after a clumsy operation? It was, perhaps, only a choice of deaths!"

'Mr Morgan had been stung at all this. Perhaps I did not speak quite respectfully enough: I was a good deal excited. We only got more and more angry with each other; though he, to do him justice, was as civil as could be all the time, thinking that thereby he concealed his vexation and disappointment. He did not try to conceal his anxiety about poor John. I went home weary and dispirited. I made up and took the necessary applications to John; and, promising to return with the dawn of day (I would fain have stayed, but I did not wish him to be alarmed about himself), I went home, and resolved to sit up and study the treatment of similar cases.

'Mrs Rose knocked at the door.

'"Come in!" said I sharply.

'She said she had seen I had something on my mind all day, and she could not go to bed without asking if there was nothing she could do. She was good and kind; and I could not help telling her a little of the truth. She listened pleasantly; and I shook her warmly by the hand, thinking that though she might not be very wise, her good heart made her worth a dozen keen, sharp, hard people, like Miss Horsman.

'When I went at daybreak, I saw John's wife for a few minutes outside the door. She seemed to wish her husband had been in Mr Morgan's hands rather than mine; but she gave me as good an account as I dared to hope for of the manner in which her husband had passed the night. This was confirmed by my own examination.

'When Mr Morgan and I visited him together later on in the day, John said what we had agreed upon the day before; and I told Mr Morgan openly that it was by my advice that amputation was declined. He did not speak to me till we had left the house. Then he said – "Now, sir, from this time, I consider this case entirely in your hands. Only remember the poor fellow has a wife and six children.

In case you come round to my opinion, remember that Mr White could come over, as he has done before, for the operation."

'So Mr Morgan believed I declined operating because I felt myself incapable! Very well! I was much mortified.

'An hour after we parted, I received a note to this effect:

> *DEAR SIR, I will take the long round today, to leave you at liberty to attend to Brouncker's case, which I feel to be a very responsible one.*
>
> *J. MORGAN*

'This was kindly done. I went back, as soon as I could, to John's cottage. While I was in the inner room with him, I heard the Miss Tomkinsons' voices outside. They had called to enquire. Miss Tomkinson came in, and evidently was poking and snuffing about. (Mrs Brouncker told her that I was within; and within I resolved to be till they had gone.)

'"What is this close smell?" asked she. "I am afraid you are not cleanly. Cheese! – cheese in this cupboard! No wonder there is an unpleasant smell. Don't you know how particular you should be about being clean when there is illness about?"

'Mrs Brouncker was exquisitely clean in general, and was piqued at these remarks.

'"If you please, ma'am, I could not leave John yesterday to do any housework, and Jenny put the dinner things away. She is but eight years old."

'But this did not satisfy Miss Tomkinson, who was evidently pursuing the course of her observations.

'"Fresh butter, I declare! Well now, Mrs Brouncker, do you know I don't allow myself fresh butter at this time of the year? How can you save, indeed, with such extravagance!"

'"Please, ma'am," answered Mrs Brouncker, "you'd think it strange, if I was to take such liberties in your house as you're taking here."

'I expected to hear a sharp answer. No! Miss Tomkinson liked plain-speaking. The only person in whom she would tolerate round-about ways of talking was her sister.

'"Well, that's true," she said. "Still, you must not be above taking advice. Fresh butter is extravagant at this time of the year. However, you're a good kind of woman, and I've a great respect for John. Send Jenny for some broth as soon as he can take it. Come, Caroline, we have got to go on to Williams's."

'But Miss Caroline said that she was tired, and would rest where she was till Miss Tomkinson came back. I was a prisoner for some time, I found. When she was alone with Mrs Brouncker, she said:

'"You must not be hurt by my sister's abrupt manner. She means well. She has not much imagination or sympathy, and cannot understand the distraction of mind produced by the illness of a worshipped husband." I could hear the loud sigh of commiseration which followed this speech. Mrs Brouncker said:

'"Please, ma'am, I don't worship my husband. I would not be so wicked."

'"Goodness! You don't think it wicked, do you? For my part, if... I should worship, I should adore him." I thought she need not imagine such improbable cases. But sturdy Mrs Brouncker said again: "I hope I know my duty better. I've not learned my Commandments for nothing. I know Whom I ought to worship."

'Just then the children came in, dirty and unwashed, I have no doubt. And now Miss Caroline's real nature peeped out. She spoke sharply to them, and asked them if they had no manners, little pigs as they were, to come brushing against her silk gown in that way? She sweetened herself again, and was as sugary as love when Miss Tomkinson returned to her, accompanied by one whose voice, "like winds in summer sighing", I knew to be my dear Sophy's.

'She did not say much; but what she did say, and the manner in which she spoke, was tender and compassionate in the highest degree; and she came to take the four little ones back with her to the vicarage, in order that they might be out of their mother's way; the older two might help at home. She offered to wash their hands and faces; and when I emerged from my inner chamber, after the Miss Tomkinsons had left, I found her with a chubby child on her knees, bubbling and spluttering against her white wet hand, with a face bright, rosy, and merry under the operation. Just as I came in, she said to him, "There, Jemmy, now I can kiss you with this nice clean face."

'She coloured when she saw me. I liked her speaking, and I liked her silence. She was silent now, and I "lo'ed her a' the better". I gave my directions to Mrs Brouncker, and hastened to overtake Sophy and the children; but they had gone round by the lanes, I suppose, for I saw nothing of them.

'I was very anxious about the case. At night I went again. Miss Horsman had been there; I believe she was really kind among the poor, but she could not help leaving a sting behind her everywhere. She had been frightening Mrs Brouncker about her husband, and been, I have no doubt, expressing her doubts of my skill; for Mrs Brouncker began:

'"Oh, please, sir, if you'll only let Mr Morgan take off his arm, I will never think the worse of you for not being able to do it."

'I told her it was from no doubt of my own competency to perform the operation that I wished to save the arm; but that he himself was anxious to have it spared.

"'Ay, bless him! he frets about not earning enough to keep us, if he's crippled; but, sir, I don't care about that. I would work my fingers to the bone, and so would the children; I'm sure we'd be proud to do for him, and keep him; God bless him! it would be far better to have him only with one arm, than to have him in the churchyard, Miss Horsman says –"

"'Confound Miss Horsman!" said I.

"'Thank you, Mr Harrison," said her well-known voice behind me. She had come out, dark as it was, to bring some old linen to Mrs Brouncker; for, as I said before, she was very kind to all the poor people of Duncombe.

"'I beg your pardon'; for I really was sorry for my speech – or rather that she had heard it.

"'There is no occasion for any apology," she replied, drawing herself up, and pinching her lips into a very venomous shape.

'John was doing pretty well; but of course the danger of lockjaw was not over. Before I left, his wife entreated me to take off the arm; she wrung her hands in her passionate entreaty. "Spare him to me, Mr Harrison," she implored. Miss Horsman stood by. It was mortifying enough; but I thought of the power which was in my hands, as I firmly believed, of saving the limb; and I was inflexible.

'You cannot think how pleasantly Mrs Rose's sympathy came in on my return. To be sure she did not understand one word of the case, which I detailed to her; but she listened with interest, and, as long as she held her tongue, I thought she was really taking it in; but her first remark was as *mal-àpropos* as could be.

"'You are anxious to save the tibia – I see completely how difficult that will be. My late husband had a case exactly similar, and I remember his anxiety; but you must not distress yourself too much, my dear Mr Harrison; I have no doubt it will end well."

'I knew she had no grounds for this assurance, and yet it comforted me.

'However, as it happened, John did fully as well as I could have hoped for; of course, he was long in rallying his strength; and, indeed, sea air was evidently so necessary for his complete restoration, that I accepted with gratitude Mrs Rose's proposal of sending him to Highport for a fortnight or three weeks. Her kind generosity in this matter made me more desirous than ever of paying her every mark of respect and attention.

CHAPTER XV

'About this time there was a sale at Ashmeadow, a pretty house in the neighbourhood of Duncombe. It was likewise an easy walk, and the spring days tempted many people thither, who had no intention of buying anything, but who liked the idea of rambling through the woods, gay with early primroses and wild daffodils, and of seeing the gardens and house, which till now had been shut up from the ingress of the townspeople. Mrs Rose had planned to go, but an unlucky cold prevented her. She begged me to bring her a very particular account, saying she delighted in details, and always questioned Mr Rose as to the side dishes of the dinners to which he went. The late Mr Rose's conduct was always held up as a model to me, by the way. I walked to Ashmeadow, pausing or loitering with different parties of townspeople, all bound in the same direction. At last I found the Vicar and Sophy, and with them I stayed. I sat by Sophy and talked and listened. A sale is a very pleasant gathering after all. The auctioneer, in a country place, is privileged to joke from his rostrum, and, having a personal knowledge of most of the people, can sometimes make a very keen hit at their circum-stances, and turn the laugh against them. For instance, on the present occasion, there was a farmer present, with his wife, who was notoriously the grey mare. The auctioneer was selling some horse-cloths, and called out to recommend the article to her, telling her, with a knowing look at the company, that they would make her a dashing pair of trousers, if she was in want of such an article. She drew herself up with dignity, and said, "Come, John, we've had enough of this." Whereupon there was a burst of laughter, and in the midst of it John meekly followed his wife out of the place. The furniture in the sitting rooms was, I believe, very beautiful, but I did not notice it much. Suddenly I heard the auctioneer speaking to me, "Mr Harrison, won't you give me a bid for this table?"

'It was a very pretty little table of walnut-wood. I thought it would go into my study very well, so I gave him a bid. I saw Miss Horsman bidding against me, so I went off with a full force, and at last it was knocked down to me. The auctioneer smiled, and congratulated me.

'"A most useful present for Mrs Harrison, when that lady comes."

'Everybody laughed. They like a joke about marriage; it is so easy to comprehend. But the table which I had thought was for writing, turned out to be a work-table, scissors and thimble complete. No wonder I looked foolish. Sophy was not looking at me, that was one comfort. She was busy arranging a nosegay of wood-anemone and wild sorrel.

'Miss Horsman came up, with her curious eyes.

'"I had no idea things were far enough advanced for you to be purchasing a work-table, Mr Harrison."

'I laughed off my awkwardness.

'"Did not you, Miss Horsman? You are very much behind-hand. You have not heard of my piano, then?"

'"No, indeed," she said, half uncertain whether I was serious or not. "Then it seems there is nothing wanting but the lady."

'"Perhaps she may not be wanting either," said I; for I wished to perplex her keen curiosity.

CHAPTER XVI

'When I got home from my round, I found Mrs Rose in some sorrow.

'"Miss Horsman called after you left," said she. "Have you heard how John Brouncker is at Highport?"

'"Very well," replied I. "I called on his wife just now, and she had just got a letter from him. She had been anxious about him, for she had not heard for a week. However, all's right now; and she has pretty well enough of work, at Mrs Munton's, as her servant is ill. Oh, they'll do, never fear."

'"At Mrs Munton's? Oh, that accounts for it, then. She is so deaf, and makes such blunders."

'"Accounts for what?" said I.

'"Oh, perhaps I had better not tell you," hesitated Mrs Rose.

'"Yes, tell me at once. I beg your pardon, but I hate mysteries."

'"You are so like my poor dear Mr Rose. He used to speak to me just in that sharp, cross way. It is only that Miss Horsman called. She had been making a collection for John Brouncker's widow and –"

'"But the man's alive!" said I.

'"So it seems. But Mrs Munton had told her that he was dead. And she has got Mr Morgan's name down at the head of the list, and Mr Bullock's."

'Mr Morgan and I had got into a short, cool way of speaking to each other ever since we had differed so much about the treatment of Brouncker's arm; and I had heard once or twice of his shakes of the head over John's case. He would not have spoken against my method for the world, and fancied that he concealed his fears.

'"Miss Horsman is very ill-natured, I think," sighed forth Mrs Rose.

'I saw that something had been said of which I had not heard, for the mere fact of collecting money for the widow was good-natured, whoever did it; so I asked, quietly, what she had said.

'"Oh, I don't know if I should tell you. I only know she made me cry; for I'm not well, and I can't bear to hear anyone that I live with abused."

'Come! this was pretty plain.

'"What did Miss Horsman say of me?" asked I, half laughing, for I knew there was no love lost between us.

'"Oh, she only said she wondered you could go to sales, and spend your money there, when your ignorance had made Jane Brouncker a widow, and her children fatherless."

'"Pooh! pooh! John's alive, and likely to live as long as you or I, thanks to you, Mrs Rose."

'When my work-table came home, Mrs Rose was so struck with its beauty and completeness, and I was so much obliged to her for her identification of my interests with hers, and the kindness of her whole conduct about John, that I begged her to accept of it. She seemed very much pleased; and, after a few apologies, she consented to take it, and placed it in the most conspicuous part of the front parlour, where she usually sat. There was a good deal of morning calling in Duncombe after the sale, and during this time the fact of John being alive was established to the conviction of all except Miss Horsman, who, I believe, still doubted. I myself told Mr Morgan, who immediately went to reclaim his money; saying to me that he was thankful for the information; he was truly glad to hear it; and he shook me warmly by the hand for the first time for a month.

CHAPTER XVII

'A few days after the sale, I was in the consulting room. The servant must have left the folding-doors a little ajar, I think. Mrs Munton came to call on Mrs Rose; and the former being deaf, I heard all the speeches of the latter lady, as she was obliged to speak very loud in order to be heard. She began:

'"This is a great pleasure, Mrs Munton, so seldom as you are well enough to go out."

'Mumble, mumble, mumble, through the door.

'"Oh, very well, thank you. Take this seat, and then you can admire my new work-table, ma'am; a present from Mr Harrison."

'Mumble, mumble.

'"Who could have told you, ma'am? Miss Horsman? Oh, yes, I showed it Miss Horsman."

'Mumble, mumble.

'"I don't quite understand you, ma'am."

'Mumble, mumble.

'"I'm not blushing, I believe. I really am quite in the dark as to what you mean."

'Mumble, mumble.

'"Oh, yes, Mr Harrison and I are most comfortable together. He reminds me so of my dear Mr Rose – just as fidgety and anxious in his profession."

'Mumble, mumble.

'"I'm sure you are joking now, ma'am." Then I heard a pretty loud:

'"Oh, no"; mumble, mumble, mumble, for a long time.

'"Did he really? Well, I'm sure I don't know. I should be sorry to think he was doomed to be unfortunate in so serious an affair; but you know my undying regard for the late Mr Rose."

'Another long mumble.

'"You're very kind, I'm sure. Mr Rose always thought more of my happiness than his own" – a little crying – "but the turtle-dove has always been my ideal, ma'am."

'Mumble, mumble.

'"No one could have been happier than I. As you say, it is a compliment to matrimony."

'Mumble.

'"Oh, but you must not repeat such a thing! Mr Harrison would not like it. He can't bear to have his affairs spoken about."

'Then there was a change of subject; an enquiry after some poor person, I imagine. I heard Mrs Rose say:

'"She has got a mucous membrane, I'm afraid, ma'am."

'A commiserating mumble.

'"Not always fatal. I believe Mr Rose knew some cases that lived for years after it was discovered that they had a mucous membrane." A pause. Then Mrs Rose spoke in a different tone.

'"Are you sure, ma'am, there is no mistake about what he said?"

'Mumble.

'"Pray don't be so observant, Mrs Munton; you find out too much. One can have no little secrets."

'The call broke up; and I heard Mrs Munton say in the passage, "I wish you joy, ma'am, with all my heart. There's no use denying it; for I've seen all along what would happen."

'When I went in to dinner, I said to Mrs Rose:

'"You've had Mrs Munton here, I think. Did she bring any news?" To my surprise, she bridled and simpered, and replied, "Oh, you must not ask, Mr Harrison; such foolish reports."

'I did not ask, as she seemed to wish me not, and I knew there were silly reports always about. Then I think she was vexed that

I did not ask. Altogether she went on so strangely that I could not help looking at her; and then she took up a hand-screen, and held it between me and her. I really felt rather anxious.

"'Are you not feeling well?" said I innocently.

"'Oh, thank you, I believe I'm quite well; only the room is rather warm, is it not?"

"'Let me put the blinds down for you? the sun begins to have a good deal of power." I drew down the blinds.

"'You are so attentive, Mr Harrison. Mr Rose himself never did more for my little wishes than you do."

"'I wish I could do more – I wish I could show you how much I feel" – her kindness to John Brouncker, I was going on to say; but I was just then called out to a patient. Before I went I turned back, and said:

"'Take care of yourself, my dear Mrs Rose; you had better rest a little."

"'For your sake, I will," said she tenderly.

'I did not care for whose sake she did it. Only I really thought she was not quite well, and required rest. I thought she was more affected than usual at teatime; and could have been angry with her nonsensical ways once or twice, but that I knew the real goodness of her heart. She said she wished she had the power to sweeten my life as she could my tea. I told her what a comfort she had been during my late time of anxiety; and then I stole out to try if I could hear the evening singing at the vicarage, by standing close to the garden wall.

CHAPTER XVIII

'The next morning I met Mr Bullock by appointment to talk a little about the legacy which was paid into his hands. As I was leaving his office, feeling full of my riches, I met Miss Horsman. She smiled rather grimly, and said:

'"Oh, Mr Harrison, I must congratulate you, I believe. I don't know whether I ought to have known, but as I do, I must wish you joy. A very nice little sum, too. I always said you would have money."

'So she had found out my legacy, had she? Well, it was no secret, and one likes the reputation of being a person of property. Accordingly I smiled, and said I was much obliged to her; and, if I could alter the figures to my liking, she might congratulate me still more.

'She said, "Oh, Mr Harrison, you can't have everything. It would be better the other way, certainly. Money is the great thing, as you've found out. The relation died most opportunely, I must say."

'"He was no relative," said I; "only an intimate friend."

'"Dear-ah-me! I thought it had been a brother! Well, at any rate, the legacy is safe."

'I wished her good morning, and passed on. Before long I was sent for to Miss Tomkinson's.

'Miss Tomkinson sat in severe state to receive me. I went in with an air of ease, because I always felt so uncomfortable.

'"Is this true that I hear?" asked she, in an inquisitorial manner.

'I thought she alluded to my five hundred pounds; so I smiled, and said that I believed it was.

'"Can money be so great an object with you, Mr Harrison?" she asked again.

'I said I had never cared much for money, except as an assistance to any plan of settling in life; and then, as I did not like her severe way of treating the subject, I said that I hoped everyone was well; though of course I expected someone was ill, or I should not have been sent for.

'Miss Tomkinson looked very grave and sad. Then she answered: "Caroline is very poorly – the old palpitations at the heart; but of course that is nothing to you."

'I said I was sorry. She had a weakness there, I knew. Could I see her? I might be able to order something for her.

'I thought I heard Miss Tomkinson say something in a low voice about my being a heartless deceiver. Then she spoke up. "I was always distrustful of you, Mr Harrison. I never liked your looks. I begged Caroline again and again not to confide in you. I foresaw how it would end. And now I fear her precious life will be a sacrifice."

'I begged her not to distress herself, for in all probability there was very little the matter with her sister. Might I see her?

'"No!" she said shortly, standing up as if to dismiss me. "There has been too much of this seeing and calling. By my consent, you shall never see her again."

'I bowed. I was annoyed, of course. Such a dismissal might injure my practice just when I was most anxious to increase it.

'"Have you no apology, no excuse to offer?"

'I said I had done my best; I did not feel that there was any reason to offer an apology. I wished her good morning. Suddenly she came forwards.

'"Oh, Mr Harrison," said she, "if you have really loved Caroline, do not let a little paltry money make you desert her for another."

'I was struck dumb. Loved Miss Caroline! I loved Miss Tomkinson a great deal better, and yet I disliked her. She went on: "'I have saved nearly three thousand pounds. If you think you are too poor to marry without money, I will give it all to Caroline. I am strong, and can go on working; but she is weak, and this disappointment will kill her." She sat down suddenly, and covered her face with her hands. Then she looked up.

"'You are unwilling, I see. Don't suppose I would have urged you if it had been for myself; but she has had so much sorrow." And now she fairly cried aloud. I tried to explain; but she would not listen, but kept saying, "Leave the house, sir! leave the house!" But I would be heard.

"'I have never had any feeling warmer than respect for Miss Caroline, and I have never shown any different feeling. I never for an instant thought of making her my wife, and she has had no cause in my behaviour to imagine I entertained any such intention."

"'This is adding insult to injury," said she. "Leave the house, sir, this instant!"

CHAPTER XIX

'I went, and sadly enough. In a small town such an occurrence is sure to be talked about, and to make a great deal of mischief. When I went home to dinner I was so full of it, and foresaw so clearly that I should need some advocate soon to set the case in its right light, that I determined on making a confidante of good Mrs Rose. I could not eat. She watched me tenderly, and sighed when she saw my want of appetite.

'"I am sure you have something on your mind, Mr Harrison. Would it be – would it not be – a relief to impart it to some sympathising friend?"

'It was just what I wanted to do.

'"My dear, kind Mrs Rose," said I, "I must tell you, if you will listen."

'She took up the fire-screen, and held it, as yesterday, between me and her.

'"The most unfortunate misunderstanding has taken place. Miss Tomkinson thinks that I have been paying attentions to Miss Caroline; when, in fact – may I tell you, Mrs Rose? – my affections are placed elsewhere. Perhaps you have found it out already?" for indeed I thought I had been too much in love to conceal my attachment to Sophy from anyone who knew my movements as well as Mrs Rose.

'She hung down her head, and said she believed she had found out my secret.

'"Then only think how miserably I am situated. If I have any hope – oh, Mrs Rose, do you think I have any hope –"

'She put the hand-screen still more before her face, and after some hesitation she said she thought, "If I persevered – in time – I might have hope." And then she suddenly got up, and left the room.

CHAPTER XX

'That afternoon I met Mr Bullock in the street. My mind was so full of the affair with Miss Tomkinson that I should have passed him without notice, if he had not stopped me short, and said that he must speak to me; about my wonderful five hundred pounds, I supposed. But I did not care for that now.

'"What is this I hear," said he severely, "about your engagement with Mrs Rose?"

'"With Mrs Rose!" said I, almost laughing, although my heart was heavy enough.

'"Yes! with Mrs Rose!" said he sternly.

'"I'm not engaged to Mrs Rose," I replied. "There is some mistake."

'"I'm glad to hear it, sir," he answered, "very glad. It requires some explanation, however. Mrs Rose has been congratulated, and has acknowledged the truth of the report. It is confirmed by many facts. The work-table you bought, confessing your intention of giving it to your future wife, is given to her. How do you account for these things, sir?"

'I said I did not pretend to account for them. At present a good deal was inexplicable; and, when I could give an explanation, I did not think that I should feel myself called upon to give it to him.

'"Very well, sir; very well," replied he, growing very red. "I shall take care and let Mr Morgan know the opinion I entertain of you. What do you think that man deserves to be called who enters a family under the plea of friendship, and takes advantage of his intimacy to win the affections of the daughter, and then engages himself to another woman?"

'I thought he referred to Miss Caroline. I simply said I could only say that I was not engaged; and that Miss Tomkinson had been quite mistaken in supposing I had been paying any attentions to her sister beyond those dictated by mere civility.

'"Miss Tomkinson! Miss Caroline! I don't understand to what you refer. Is there another victim to your perfidy? What I allude to are the attentions you have paid to my daughter, Miss Bullock."

'Another! I could but disclaim, as I had done in the case of Miss Caroline; but I began to be in despair. Would Miss Horsman, too, come forward as a victim to my tender affections? It was all Mr Morgan's doing, who had lectured me into this tenderly deferential manner. But, on the score of Miss Bullock, I was brave in my innocence. I had positively disliked her; and so I told her father, though in more civil and measured terms, adding that I was sure the feeling was reciprocal.

'He looked as if he would like to horsewhip me. I longed to call him out.

'"I hope my daughter has had sense enough to despise you; I hope she has, that's all, I trust my wife may be mistaken as to her feelings."

'So, he had heard all through the medium of his wife. That explained something, and rather calmed me. I begged he would ask Miss Bullock if she had ever thought I had any ulterior object in my intercourse with her, beyond mere friendliness (and not so much of that, I might have added). I would refer it to her.

'"Girls," said Mr Bullock, a little more quietly, "do not like to acknowledge that they have been deceived and disappointed. I consider my wife's testimony as likely to be nearer the truth than my daughter's, for that reason. And she tells me she never doubted but that, if not absolutely engaged, you understood each other perfectly. She is sure Jemima is deeply wounded by your engagement to Mrs Rose."

'"Once for all, I am not engaged to anybody. Till you have seen your daughter, and learnt the truth from her, I will wish you farewell."

'I bowed in a stiff, haughty manner, and walked off homewards. But when I got to my own door, I remembered Mrs Rose, and all that Mr Bullock had said about her acknowledging the truth of the report of my engagement to her. Where could I go to be safe? Mrs Rose, Miss Bullock, Miss Caroline – they lived as it were at the three points of an equilateral triangle; here was I in the centre. I would go to Mr Morgan's, and drink tea with him. There, at any rate, I was secure from anyone wanting to marry me; and I might be as professionally bland as I liked, without being misunderstood. But there, too, a *contretemps* awaited me.

CHAPTER XXI

'Mr Morgan was looking grave. After a minute or two of humming and hawing, he said:

'"I have been sent for to Miss Caroline Tomkinson, Mr Harrison. I am sorry to hear of this. I am grieved to find that there seems to have been some trifling with the affections of a very worthy lady. Miss Tomkinson, who is in sad distress, tells me that they had every reason to believe that you were attached to her sister. May I ask if you do not intend to marry her?"

'I said, nothing was farther from my thoughts.

'"My dear sir," said Mr Morgan, rather agitated, "do not express yourself so strongly and vehemently. It is derogatory to the sex to speak so. It is more respectful to say, in these cases, that you do not venture to entertain a hope; such a manner is generally understood, and does not sound like such positive objection."

'"I cannot help it, sir; I must talk in my own natural manner. I would not speak disrespectfully to any woman; but nothing should induce me to marry Miss Caroline Tomkinson; not if she were Venus herself, and Queen of England into the bargain. I cannot understand what has given rise to the idea."

'"Indeed, sir; I think that is very plain. You have a trifling case to attend to in the house, and you invariably make it a pretext for seeing and conversing with the lady."

'"That was her doing, not mine!" said I vehemently.

'"Allow me to go on. You are discovered on your knees before her – a positive injury to the establishment as Miss Tomkinson observes; a most passionate valentine is sent; and, when questioned, you acknowledge the sincerity of meaning which you affix to such things." He stopped; for in his earnestness he had been talking more than usual, and was out of breath. I burst in with my explanations:

"'The valentine I know nothing about.'

"'It is in your handwriting,' said he coldly. 'I should be most deeply grieved to – in fact, I will not think it possible of your father's son. But I must say, it is in your handwriting.'

'I tried again, and at last succeeded in convincing him that I had been only unfortunate, not intentionally guilty of winning Miss Caroline's affections. I said that I had been endeavouring, it was true, to practise the manner he had recommended, of universal sympathy, and recalled to his mind some of the advice he had given me. He was a good deal hurried.

"'But, my dear sir, I had no idea that you would carry it out to such consequences. 'Philandering', Miss Tomkinson called it. That is a hard word, sir. My manner has been always tender and sympathetic; but I am not aware that I ever excited any hopes; there never was any report about me. I believe no lady was ever attached to me. You must strive after this happy medium, sir.'

'I was still distressed. Mr Morgan had only heard of one, but there were three ladies (including Miss Bullock) hoping to marry me. He saw my annoyance.

"'Don't be too much distressed about it, my dear sir; I was sure you were too honourable a man, from the first. With a conscience like yours, I would defy the world.'

'He became anxious to console me, and I was hesitating whether I would not tell him all my three dilemmas, when a note was brought in to him. It was from Mrs Munton. He threw it to me, with a face of dismay.

MY DEAR MR MORGAN, I most sincerely congratulate you on the happy matrimonial engagement I hear you have formed with Miss Tomkinson. All previous circumstances, as I have just been remarking to Miss Horsman, combine to promise you felicity. And I wish that every blessing may attend your married life. – Most sincerely yours,

JANE MUNTON

'I could not help laughing, he had been so lately congratulating himself that no report of the kind had ever been circulated about himself. He said:

"'Sir! this is no laughing matter; I assure you it is not."

'I could not resist asking, if I was to conclude that there was no truth in the report.

"'Truth, sir! it's a lie from beginning to end. I don't like to speak too decidedly about any lady; and I've a great respect for Miss Tomkinson; but I do assure you, sir, I'd as soon marry one of Her Majesty's Life Guards. I would rather; it would be more suitable. Miss Tomkinson is a very worthy lady; but she's a perfect grenadier."

'He grew very nervous. He was evidently insecure. He thought it not impossible that Miss Tomkinson might come and marry him, *vi et armis*. I am sure he had some dim idea of abduction in his mind. Still, he was better off than I was; for he was in his own house, and report had only engaged him to one lady; while I stood, like Paris, among three contending beauties. Truly, an apple of discord had been thrown into our little town. I suspected at the time, what I know now, that it was Miss Horsman's doing; not intentionally, I will do her the justice to say. But she had shouted out the story of my behaviour to Miss Caroline up Mrs Munton's trumpet; and that lady, possessed with the idea that I was engaged to Mrs Rose, had imagined the masculine pronoun to relate to Mr Morgan, whom she had seen only that afternoon tête-à-tête with Miss Tomkinson, condoling with her in some tender deferential manner, I'll be bound.

CHAPTER XXII

'I was very cowardly. I positively dared not go home; but at length I was obliged to. I had done all I could to console Mr Morgan, but he refused to be comforted. I went at last. I rang at the bell. I don't know who opened the door, but I think it was Mrs Rose. I kept a handkerchief to my face, and, muttering something about having a dreadful toothache, I flew up to my room and bolted the door. I had no candle; but what did that signify. I was safe. I could not sleep; and when I did fall into a sort of doze, it was ten times worse wakening up. I could not remember whether I was engaged or not. If I was engaged, who was the lady? I had always considered myself as rather plain than otherwise; but surely I had made a mistake. Fascinating I certainly must be; but perhaps I was handsome. As soon as day dawned, I got up to ascertain the fact at the looking-glass. Even with the best disposition to be convinced, I could not see any striking beauty in my round face, with an unshaven beard and a nightcap like a fool's cap at the top. No! I must be content to be plain, but agreeable. All this I tell you in confidence. I would not have my little bit of vanity known for the world. I fell asleep towards morning. I was awakened by a tap at my door. It was Peggy: she put in a hand with a note. I took it.

'"It is not from Miss Horsman?" said I, half in joke, half in very earnest fright.

'"No, sir; Mr Morgan's man brought it."

'I opened it. It ran thus:

MY DEAR SIR, It is now nearly twenty years since I have had a little relaxation, and I find that my health requires it. I have also the utmost confidence in you, and I am sure this feeling is shared by our patients. I have, therefore, no scruple in putting in execution a hastily-formed plan, and going to Chesterton to catch the early train on my way to Paris. If your accounts are good, I shall remain away probably a fortnight. Direct to Meurice's. – Yours most truly,

J. MORGAN

P.S. – Perhaps it may be as well not to name where I am gone, especially to Miss Tomkinson.

'He had deserted me. He – with only one report – had left me to stand my ground with three.

'"Mrs Rose's kind regards, sir, and it's nearly nine o'clock. Breakfast has been ready this hour, sir."

'"Tell Mrs Rose I don't want any breakfast. Or stay" (for I was very hungry), "I will take a cup of tea and some toast up here."

'Peggy brought the tray to the door.

'"I hope you're not ill, sir?" said she kindly.

'"Not very, I shall be better when I get into the air."

'"Mrs Rose seems sadly put about," said she; "she seems so grieved like."

'I watched my opportunity, and went out by the side door in the garden.

CHAPTER XXIII

'I had intended to ask Mr Morgan to call at the vicarage, and give his parting explanation before they could hear the report. Now I thought that, if I could see Sophy, I would speak to her myself; but I did not wish to encounter the Vicar. I went along the lane at the back of the vicarage, and came suddenly upon Miss Bullock. She coloured, and asked me if I would allow her to speak to me. I could only be resigned; but I thought I could probably set one report at rest by this conversation.

'She was almost crying.

'"I must tell you, Mr Harrison, I have watched you here in order to speak to you. I heard with the greatest regret of papa's conversation with you yesterday." She was fairly crying. "I believe Mrs Bullock finds me in her way, and wants to have me married. It is the only way in which I can account for such a complete misrepresentation as she had told papa. I don't care for you, in the least, sir. You never paid me any attentions. You've been almost rude to me; and I have liked you the better. That's to say, I never have liked you."

'"I am truly glad to hear what you say," answered I. "Don't distress yourself. I was sure there was some mistake."

'But she cried bitterly.

'"It is so hard to feel that my marriage – my absence – is desired so earnestly at home. I dread every new acquaintance we form with any gentleman. It is sure to be the beginning of a series of attacks on him, of which everybody must be aware, and to which they may think I am a willing party. But I should not much mind if it were not for the conviction that she wishes me so earnestly away. Oh, my own dear mamma, you would never –"

'She cried more than ever. I was truly sorry for her, and had just taken her hand, and began – "My dear Miss Bullock" – when the door in the wall of the vicarage garden opened. It was the Vicar letting out Miss Tomkinson, whose face was all swelled with crying. He saw me; but he did not bow, or make any sign. On the contrary, he looked down as from a severe eminence, and shut the door hastily. I turned to Miss Bullock.

'"I am afraid the Vicar has been hearing something to my disadvantage from Miss Tomkinson, and it is very awkward" – she finished my sentence – "To have found us here together. Yes; but, as long as we understand that we do not care for each other, it does not signify what people say."

'"Oh, but to me it does," said I. "I may, perhaps, tell you – but do not mention it to a creature – I am attached to Miss Hutton."

'"To Sophy! Oh, Mr Harrison, I am so glad; she is such a sweet creature. Oh, I wish you joy."

'"Not yet; I have never spoken about it."

'"Oh, but it is certain to happen." She jumped with a woman's rapidity to a conclusion. And then she began to praise Sophy. Never was a man yet who did not like to hear the praises of his mistress. I walked by her side; we came past the front of the vicarage together. I looked up, and saw Sophy there, and she saw me.

'That afternoon she was sent away – sent to visit her aunt ostensibly; in reality, because of the reports of my conduct, which were showered down upon the Vicar, and one of which he saw confirmed by his own eyes.

CHAPTER XXIV

'I heard of Sophy's departure as one heard of everything, soon after it had taken place. I did not care for the awkwardness of my situation, which had so perplexed and amused me in the morning. I felt that something was wrong; that Sophy was taken away from me. I sank into despair. If anybody liked to marry me, they might. I was willing to be sacrificed. I did not speak to Mrs Rose. She wondered at me, and grieved over my coldness, I saw; but I had left off feeling anything. Miss Tomkinson cut me in the street; and it did not break my heart. Sophy was gone away; that was all I cared for. Where had they sent her to? Who was her aunt that she should go and visit her? One day I met Lizzie, who looked as though she had been told not to speak to me; but I could not help doing so.

'"Have your heard from your sister?" said I.

'"Yes."

'"Where is she? I hope she is well."

'"She is at the Leoms'" – I was not much wiser. "Oh, yes, she is very well. Fanny says she was at the Assembly last Wednesday, and danced all night with the officers."

'I thought I would enter myself a member of the Peace Society at once. She was a little flirt, and a hard-hearted creature. I don't think I wished Lizzie goodbye.

CHAPTER XXV

'What most people would have considered a more serious evil than Sophy's absence, befell me. I found that my practice was falling off. The prejudice of the town ran strongly against me. Mrs Munton told me all that was said. She heard it through Miss Horsman. It was said – cruel little town – that my negligence or ignorance had been the cause of Walter's death; that Miss Tyrrell had become worse under my treatment; and that John Brouncker was all but dead, if he was not quite, from my mismanagement. All Jack Marshland's jokes and revelations, which had, I thought, gone to oblivion, were raked up to my discredit. He himself, formerly, to my astonishment, rather a favourite with the good people of Duncombe, was spoken of as one of my disreputable friends.

'In short, so prejudiced were the good people of Duncombe that I believe a very little would have made them suspect me of a brutal highway robbery, which took place in the neighbourhood about this time. Mrs Munton told me, *à propos* of the robbery, that she had never yet understood the cause of my year's imprisonment in Newgate; she had no doubt, from what Mr Morgan had told her, there was some good reason for it; but if I would tell her the particulars, she should like to know them.

'Miss Tomkinson sent for Mr White, from Chesterton, to see Miss Caroline; and, as he was coming over, all our old patients seemed to take advantage of it, and send for him too.

'But the worst of all was the Vicar's manner to me. If he had cut me, I could have asked him why he did so. But the freezing change in his behaviour was indescribable, though bitterly felt. I heard of Sophy's gaiety from Lizzie. I thought of writing to her. Just then Mr Morgan's fortnight of absence expired. I was wearied out by Mrs Rose's tender vagaries, and took no comfort from her sympathy, which indeed I rather avoided. Her tears irritated, instead of grieving me. I wished I could tell her at once that I had no intention of marrying her.

CHAPTER XXVI

'Mr Morgan had not been at home above two hours before he was sent for to the vicarage. Sophy had come back, and I had never heard of it. She had come home ill and weary, and longing for rest: and the rest seemed approaching with awful strides. Mr Morgan forgot all his Parisian adventures, and all his terror of Miss Tomkinson, when he was sent for to see her. She was ill of a fever, which made fearful progress. When he told me, I wished to force the vicarage door, if I might but see her. But I controlled myself, and only cursed my weak indecision, which had prevented my writing to her. It was well I had no patients: they would have had but a poor chance of attention. I hung about Mr Morgan, who might see her, and did see her. But, from what he told me, I perceived that the measures he was adopting were powerless to check so sudden and violent an illness. Oh! if they would but let me see her! But that was out of the question. It was not merely that the Vicar had heard of my character as a gay Lothario, but that doubts had been thrown out of my medical skill. The accounts grew worse. Suddenly my resolution was taken. Mr Morgan's very regard for Sophy made him more than usually timid in his practice. I had my horse saddled, and galloped to Chesterton. I took the express train to town. I went to Dr —. I told him every particular of the case. He listened; but shook his head. He wrote down a prescription, and recommended a new preparation, not yet in full use – a preparation of a poison, in fact.

'"It may save her," said he. "It is a chance, in such a state of things as you describe. It must be given on the fifth day, if the pulse will bear it. Crabbe makes up the preparation most skilfully. Let me hear from you, I beg."

'I went to Crabbe's; I begged to make it up myself; but my hands trembled, so that I could not weigh the quantities. I asked the young man to do it for me. I went, without touching food, to the station, with my medicine and my prescription in my pocket. Back we flew through the country. I sprang on Bay Maldon, which my groom had in waiting, and galloped across the country to Duncombe.

'But I drew bridle when I came to the top of the hill – the hill above the old hall, from which we catch the first glimpse of the town, for I thought within myself that she might be dead; and I dreaded to come near certainty. The hawthorns were out in the woods, the young lambs were in the meadows, the song of the thrushes filled the air; but it only made the thought the more terrible.

'"What if, in this world of hope and life, she lies dead!" I heard the church bells soft and clear. I sickened to listen. Was it the passing bell? No! it was ringing eight o'clock. I put spurs to my horse, down hill as it was. We dashed into the town. I turned him, saddle and bridle, into the stable-yard, and went off to Mr Morgan's.

'"Is she –" said I. "How is she?"

'"Very ill. My poor fellow, I see how it is with you. She may live – but I fear. My dear sir, I am very much afraid."

'I told him of my journey and consultation with Dr —, and showed him the prescription. His hands trembled as he put on his spectacles to read it.

'"This is a very dangerous medicine, sir," said he, with his finger under the name of the poison.

'"It is a new preparation," said I. "Dr — relies much upon it."

'"I dare not administer it," he replied. "I have never tried it. It must be very powerful. I dare not play tricks in this case."

'I believe I stamped with impatience; but it was all of no use. My journey had been in vain. The more I urged the imminent danger of the case requiring some powerful remedy, the more nervous he became.

'I told him I would throw up the partnership. I threatened him with that, though, in fact, it was only what I felt I ought to do, and had resolved upon before Sophy's illness, as I had lost the confidence of his patients. He only said:

'"I cannot help it, sir. I shall regret it for your father's sake; but I must do my duty. I dare not run the risk of giving Miss Sophy this violent medicine – a preparation of a deadly poison."

'I left him without a word. He was quite right in adhering to his own views, as I can see now; but at the time I thought him brutal and obstinate.

CHAPTER XXVII

'I went home. I spoke rudely to Mrs Rose, who awaited my return at the door. I rushed past, and locked myself in my room. I could not go to bed.

'The morning sun came pouring in, and enraged me, as everything did since Mr Morgan refused. I pulled the blind down so violently that the string broke. What did it signify? The light might come in. What was the sun to me? And then I remembered that that sun might be shining on her – dead.

'I sat down and covered my face. Mrs Rose knocked at the door. I opened it. She had never been in bed, and had been crying too.

'"Mr Morgan wants to speak to you, sir."

'I rushed back for my medicine, and went to him. He stood at the door, pale and anxious.

'"She's alive, sir," said he, "but that's all. We have sent for Dr Hamilton. I'm afraid he will not come in time. Do you know, sir, I think we should venture – with Dr —'s sanction – to give her that medicine. It is but a chance; but it is the only one, I'm afraid." He fairly cried before he had ended.

'"I've got it here," said I, setting off to walk; but he could not go so fast.

'"I beg your pardon, sir," said he, "for my abrupt refusal last night."

'"Indeed, sir," said I; "I ought much rather to beg your pardon. I was very violent."

'"Oh! never mind! never mind! Will you repeat what Dr — said?"

'I did so; and then I asked, with a meekness that astonished myself, if I might not go in and administer it.

'"No, sir," said he, "I'm afraid not. I am sure your good heart would not wish to give pain. Besides, it might agitate her, if she has any consciousness before death. In her delirium she has often mentioned your name; and, sir, I'm sure you won't name it again, as it may, in fact, be considered a professional secret; but I did hear our good Vicar speak a little strongly about you; in fact, sir, I did hear him curse you. You see the mischief it might make in the parish, I'm sure, if this were known."

'I gave him the medicine, and watched him in, and saw the door shut. I hung about the place all day. Poor and rich all came to enquire. The county people drove up in their carriages – the halt and the lame came on their crutches. Their anxiety did my heart good. Mr Morgan told me that she slept, and I watched Dr Hamilton into the house. The night came on. She slept. I watched round the house. I saw the light high up, burning still and steady. Then I saw it moved. It was the crisis, in one way or other.

CHAPTER XXVIII

'Mr Morgan came out. Good old man! The tears were running down his cheeks: he could not speak: but kept shaking my hands. I did not want words. I understood that she was better.

'"Dr Hamilton says, it was the only medicine that could have saved her. I was an old fool, sir. I beg your pardon. The Vicar shall know all. I beg your pardon, sir, if I was abrupt."

'Everything went on brilliantly from this time.

'Mr Bullock called to apologise for his mistake, and consequent upbraiding. John Brouncker came home, brave and well.

'There was still Miss Tomkinson in the ranks of the enemy; and Mrs Rose too much, I feared, in the ranks of the friends.

CHAPTER XXIX

'One night she had gone to bed, and I was thinking of going. I had been studying in the back room, where I went for refuge from her in the present position of affairs – (I read a good number of surgical books about this time, and also *Vanity Fair*) – when I heard a loud, long-continued knocking at the door, enough to waken the whole street. Before I could get it open, I heard that well-known bass of Jack Marshland's – once heard, never to be forgotten – pipe up the negro song – "Who's dat knocking at de door?" Though it was raining hard at the time, and I stood waiting to let him in, he would finish his melody in the open air; loud and clear along the street it sounded. I saw Miss Tomkinson's night-capped head emerge from a window. She called out "Police! police!"

'Now there were no police, only a rheumatic constable, in the town; but it was the custom of the ladies, when alarmed at night, to call an imaginary police, which had, they thought, an intimidating effect; but, as everyone knew the real state of the unwatched town, we did not much mind it in general. Just now, however, I wanted to regain my character. So I pulled Jack in, quavering as he entered.

'"You've spoilt a good shake," said he, "that's what you have. I'm nearly up to Jenny Lind; and you see I'm a nightingale, like her."

'We sat up late; and I don't know how it was, but I told him all my matrimonial misadventures.

'"I thought I could imitate your hand pretty well," said he. "My word! it was a flaming valentine! No wonder she thought you loved her!"

'"So that was your doing, was it? Now I'll tell you what you shall do to make up for it. You shall write me a letter confessing your hoax – a letter that I can show."

"'Give me pen and paper, my boy! you shall dictate. 'With a deeply penitent heart' – Will that do for a beginning?"

'I told him what to write; a simple, straightforward confession of his practical joke. I enclosed it in a few lines of regret that, unknown to me, any of my friends should have so acted.

CHAPTER XXX

'All this time I knew that Sophy was slowly recovering. One day I met Miss Bullock, who had seen her.

'"We have been talking about you," said she, with a bright smile; for, since she knew I disliked her, she felt quite at her ease, and could smile very pleasantly. I understood that she had been explaining the misunderstanding about herself to Sophy; so that, when Jack Marshland's note had been sent to Miss Tomkinson's, I thought myself in a fair way to have my character established in two quarters. But the third was my dilemma. Mrs Rose had really so much of my true regard for her good qualities, that I disliked the idea of a formal explanation, in which a good deal must be said on my side to wound her. We had become very much estranged ever since I had heard of this report of my engagement to her. I saw that she grieved over it. While Jack Marshland stayed with us, I felt at my ease in the presence of a third person. But he told me confidentially he durst not stay long, for fear some of the ladies should snap him up, and marry him. Indeed I myself did not think it unlikely that he would snap one of them up if he could. For when we met Miss Bullock one day, and heard her hopeful, joyous account of Sophy's progress (to whom she was a daily visitor) he asked me who that bright-looking girl was? And when I told him she was the Miss Bullock of whom I had spoken to him, he was pleased to observe that he thought I had been a great fool, and asked me if Sophy had anything like such splendid eyes. He made me repeat about Miss Bullock's unhappy circumstances at home, and then became very thoughtful – a most unusual and morbid symptom in his case.

'Soon after he went, by Mr Morgan's kind offices and explanations, I was permitted to see Sophy. I might not speak much; it was prohibited, for fear of agitating her. We talked of the weather and the flowers; and we were silent. But her little white thin hand lay in mine; and we understood each other without words. I had a long interview with the Vicar afterwards, and came away glad and satisfied.

'Mr Morgan called in the afternoon, evidently anxious, though he made no direct enquiries (he was too polite for that) to hear the result of my visit at the vicarage. I told him to give me joy. He shook me warmly by the hand, and then rubbed his own together. I thought I would consult him about my dilemma with Mrs Rose, who, I was afraid, would be deeply affected by my engagement.

'"There is only one awkward circumstance," said I – "about Mrs Rose." I hesitated how to word the fact of her having received congratulations on her supposed engagement with me, and her manifest attachment; but, before I could speak, he broke in:

'"My dear sir, you need not trouble yourself about that; she will have a home. In fact, sir," said he, reddening a little, "I thought it would, perhaps, put a stop to those reports connecting my name with Miss Tomkinson's, if I married someone else. I hoped it might prove an efficacious contradiction. And I was struck with admiration for Mrs Rose's undying memory of her late husband. Not to be prolix, I have this morning obtained Mrs Rose's consent to – to marry her, in fact, sir!" said he, jerking out the climax.

'Here was an event! Then Mr Morgan had never heard the report about Mrs Rose and me. (To this day, I think she would have taken me, if I had proposed.) So much the better.

'Marriages were in the fashion that year. Mr Bullock met me one morning, as I was going to ride with Sophy. He and I had quite got over our misunderstanding, thanks to Jemima, and were as friendly as ever. This morning he was chuckling aloud as he walked.

'"Stop, Mr Harrison!" he said, as I went quickly past. "Have you heard the news? Miss Horsman has just told me Miss Caroline has eloped with young Hoggins! She is ten years older than he is! How can her gentility like being married to a tallow-chandler? It is a very good thing for her, though", he added, in a more serious manner; "old Hoggins is very rich, and, though he's angry just now, he will soon be reconciled."

'Any vanity I might have entertained on the score of the three ladies who were, at one time, said to be captivated by my charms, was being rapidly dispersed. Soon after Mr Hoggins' marriage, I met Miss Tomkinson face to face, for the first time since our memorable conversation. She stopped me, and said:

'"Don't refuse to receive my congratulations, Mr Harrison, on your most happy engagement to Miss Hutton. I owe you an apology, too, for my behaviour when I last saw you at our house. I really did think Caroline was attached to you then; and it irritated me, I confess, in a very wrong and unjustifiable way. But I heard her telling Mr Hoggins only yesterday that she had been attached to him for years; ever since he was in pinafores, she dated it from; and when I asked her afterwards how she could say so, after her distress on hearing that false report about you and Mrs Rose, she cried, and said I never had understood her; and that the hysterics which alarmed me so much were simply caused by eating pickled cucumber. I am very sorry for my stupidity and improper way of speaking; but I hope we are friends now, Mr Harrison, for I should wish to be liked by Sophy's husband."

'Good Miss Tomkinson, to believe the substitution of indigestion for disappointed affection! I shook her warmly by the hand; and we have been all right ever since. I think I told you she is baby's godmother.

CHAPTER XXXI

'I had some difficulty in persuading Jack Marshland to be groomsman; but, when he heard all the arrangements, he came. Miss Bullock was bridesmaid. He liked us all so well, that he came again at Christmas, and was far better behaved than he had been the year before. He won golden opinions indeed. Miss Tomkinson said he was a reformed young man. We dined all together at Mr Morgan's (the Vicar wanted us to go there; but, from what Sophy told me, Helen was not confident of the mince-meat, and rather dreaded so large a party). We had a jolly day of it. Mrs Morgan was as kind and motherly as ever. Miss Horsman certainly did set out a story that the Vicar was thinking of Miss Tomkinson for his second; or else, I think, we had no other report circulated in consequence of our happy, merry Christmas Day; and it is a wonder, considering how Jack Marshland went on with Jemima.'

Here Sophy came back from putting baby to bed; and Charles wakened up.

BIOGRAPHICAL NOTE

Elizabeth Gaskell was born Elizabeth Stevenson in 1810 in London, the daughter of Unitarian parents. Her father, William Stevenson, had trained as a minister but spent the greater part of his life as a journal writer and keeper of the treasury records. Elizabeth's mother died while she was still in infancy, and the baby was then moved to Knutsford in Cheshire, where she was brought up by her maternal aunt. As a Unitarian, Elizabeth was given a good formal education, and from the ages of twelve to seventeen attended school in Barford and Stratford-upon-Avon.

In 1832 Elizabeth married a minister, Reverend William Gaskell, whom she had met during a trip to Manchester, and moved away from Knutsford. Gaskell was oppressed by the atmosphere of industrial Manchester, which was in sharp contrast to her rural upbringing, though she was struck by the social vibrancy and humanitarian demands of the burgeoning city; her religious beliefs gave her a tolerance and philanthropy that were later to underpin her writing.

Gaskell's life was primarily devoted to domestic and social responsibilities until the 1840s, when a series of personal tragedies – including the death of her baby son in 1845 – inspired her to turn to writing. Her first novel, *Mary Barton: A Tale of Manchester Life*, was published in 1848 and reflected her preoccupation with the social mores and deprivation of industrial Manchester. *Mary Barton* met with much acclaim and Gaskell was persuaded by Charles Dickens to contribute to his literary journals. Several short fictions were subsequently published including the novella *Mr Harrison's Confessions* (1851) which laid the foundations for her subsequent masterpiece, *Cranford* (1853). While much of her writing concerned Manchester, *Cranford* was a humorous and affectionate account of genteel society in a small country community, clearly based on Knutsford. Two further 'problem' novels were to follow: *Ruth* (1853) and *North and South* (1855), both of which returned to the industrialised north and focused on moral failure and the contrast between the old rural ways of life and the struggles of industrial poverty.

In 1855, following the death of her friend Charlotte Brontë, Gaskell was persuaded to write her biography. *The Life of Charlotte Brontë* was published in 1857 and is still admired today, though Gaskell herself was threatened with legal action on account of her frank views on many of the real-life characters featured. She decided to restrict her subsequent output to fiction, and produced several more novels, including the unfinished *Wives and Daughters* (published posthumously in 1866) – a novel that Henry James described as 'testifying… to the fact of her genius', and a number of volumes of short stories. Domestic, social and literary demands continued to press on Gaskell and began to cause periods of intense fatigue. She kept up her output, but in November 1865, collapsed and died.

HESPERUS PRESS

Under our three imprints, Hesperus Press publishes over 300 books by many of the greatest figures in worldwide literary history, as well as contemporary and debut authors well worth discovering.

Hesperus Classics handpicks the best of worldwide and translated literature, introducing forgotten and neglected books to new generations.

Hesperus Nova showcases quality contemporary fiction and non-fiction designed to entertain and inspire.

Hesperus Minor rediscovers well-loved children's books from the past – these are books which will bring back fond memories for adults, which they will want to share with their children and loved ones.

To find out more visit **www.hesperuspress.com**

@HesperusPress

SELECTED TITLES FROM HESPERUS PRESS

Author	Title	Foreword writer
Pietro Aretino	*The School of Whoredom*	Paul Bailey
Pietro Aretino	*The Secret Life of Nuns*	
Jane Austen	*Lesley Castle*	Zoë Heller
Jane Austen	*Love and Friendship*	Fay Weldon
Honoré de Balzac	*Colonel Chabert*	A.N. Wilson
Charles Baudelaire	*On Wine and Hashish*	Margaret Drabble
Giovanni Boccaccio	*Life of Dante*	A.N. Wilson
Charlotte Brontë	*The Spell*	
Emily Brontë	*Poems of Solitude*	Helen Dunmore
Mikhail Bulgakov	*Fatal Eggs*	Doris Lessing
Mikhail Bulgakov	*The Heart of a Dog*	A.S. Byatt
Giacomo Casanova	*The Duel*	Tim Parks
Miguel de Cervantes	*The Dialogue of the Dogs*	Ben Okri
Geoffrey Chaucer	*The Parliament of Birds*	
Anton Chekhov	*The Story of a Nobody*	Louis de Bernières
Anton Chekhov	*Three Years*	William Fiennes
Wilkie Collins	*The Frozen Deep*	
Joseph Conrad	*Heart of Darkness*	A.N. Wilson
Joseph Conrad	*The Return*	Colm Tóibín
Gabriele D'Annunzio	*The Book of the Virgins*	Tim Parks
Dante Alighieri	*The Divine Comedy: Inferno*	
Dante Alighieri	*New Life*	Louis de Bernières
Daniel Defoe	*The King of Pirates*	Peter Ackroyd
Marquis de Sade	*Incest*	Janet Street-Porter
Charles Dickens	*The Haunted House*	Peter Ackroyd
Charles Dickens	*A House to Let*	
Fyodor Dostoevsky	*The Double*	Jeremy Dyson

Fyodor Dostoevsky	Poor People	Charlotte Hobson
Alexandre Dumas	*One Thousand and One Ghosts*	
George Eliot	*Amos Barton*	Matthew Sweet
Henry Fielding	*Jonathan Wild the Great*	Peter Ackroyd
F. Scott Fitzgerald	*The Popular Girl*	Helen Dunmore
Gustave Flaubert	Memoirs of a Madman	Germaine Greer
Ugo Foscolo	*Last Letters of Jacopo Ortis*	Valerio Massimo Manfredi
Elizabeth Gaskell	*Lois the Witch*	Jenny Uglow
Théophile Gautier	*The Jinx Theseus*	Gilbert Adair
André Gide		
Johann Wolfgang von Goethe	*The Man of Fifty*	A.S. Byatt
Nikolai Gogol	*The Squabble*	Patrick McCabe
E.T.A. Hoffmann	*Mademoiselle de Scudéri*	Gilbert Adair
Victor Hugo	*The Last Day of a Condemned Man*	Libby Purves
Joris-Karl Huysmans	*With the Flow*	Simon Callow
Henry James	*In the Cage*	Libby Purves
Franz Kafka	*Metamorphosis*	Martin Jarvis
Franz Kafka	*The Trial*	Zadie Smith
John Keats	*Fugitive Poems*	Andrew Motion
Heinrich von Kleist	*The Marquise of O–*	Andrew Miller
Mikhail Lermontov	*A Hero of Our Time*	Doris Lessing
Nikolai Leskov	*Lady Macbeth of Mtsensk*	Gilbert Adair
Carlo Levi	*Words are Stones*	Anita Desai
Xavier de Maistre	*A Journey Around my Room*	Alain de Botton
André Malraux	*The Way of the Kings*	Rachel Seiffert
Katherine Mansfield	*Prelude*	William Boyd
Edgar Lee Masters	*Spoon River Anthology*	Shena Mackay
Guy de Maupassant	*Butterball*	Germaine Greer
Prosper Mérimée	*Carmen*	Philip Pullman

Sir Thomas More	*The History of King Richard III*	Sister Wendy Beckett
Sándor Petőfi	*John the Valiant*	George Szirtes
Francis Petrarch	*My Secret Book*	Germaine Greer
Luigi Pirandello	*Loveless Love*	
Edgar Allan Poe	*Eureka*	Sir Patrick Moore
Alexander Pope	*The Rape of the Lock and A Key to the Lock*	Peter Ackroyd
Antoine-François Prévost	*Manon Lescaut*	Germaine Greer
Marcel Proust	*Pleasures and Days*	A.N. Wilson
Alexander Pushkin	*Dubrovsky*	Patrick Neate
Alexander Pushkin	*Ruslan and Lyudmila*	Colm Tóibín
François Rabelais	*Pantagruel*	Paul Bailey
François Rabelais	*Gargantua*	Paul Bailey
Christina Rossetti	*Commonplace*	Andrew Motion
George Sand	*The Devil's Pool*	Victoria Glendinning
Jean-Paul Sartre	*The Wall*	Justin Cartwright
Friedrich von Schiller	*The Ghost-seer*	Martin Jarvis
Mary Shelley	*Transformation*	
Percy Bysshe Shelley	*Zastrozzi*	Germaine Greer
Stendhal	*Memoirs of an Egotist*	Doris Lessing
Robert Louis Stevenson	*Dr Jekyll and Mr Hyde*	Helen Dunmore
Theodor Storm	*The Lake of the Bees*	Alan Sillitoe
Leo Tolstoy	*The Death of Ivan Ilych*	
Leo Tolstoy	*Hadji Murat*	Colm Tóibín
Ivan Turgenev	*Faust*	Simon Callow
Mark Twain	*The Diary of Adam and Eve*	John Updike
Mark Twain	*Tom Sawyer, Detective*	
Oscar Wilde	*The Portrait of Mr W.H.*	Peter Ackroyd
Virginia Woolf	*Carlyle's House and Other Sketches*	Doris Lessing
Virginia Woolf	*Monday or Tuesday*	Scarlett Thomas
Emile Zola	*For a Night of Love*	A.N. Wilson